# Laurence eyed her questioningly.

'From my observations where you are concerned, sir, whatever you may say—and whoever you may be—the proprieties required of a true gentleman do not seem to be your strong point,' Lucinda said hotly.

'What? Not even if I told you that I was the Earl of Rainborough himself?'

'Ha!' scoffed Lucinda. 'If that is so, then I am the Queen of England. From what I have been told of the Earl of Rainborough he is a gentleman of the highest order. I am sure the two of you are worlds apart.'

**Helen Dickson** was born and still lives in South Yorkshire with her husband and two sons on a busy arable farm where she combines writing with keeping a chaotic farmhouse. An incurable romantic, she writes for pleasure, owing much of her inspiration to the beauty of the countryside. She enjoys reading and music; history has always captivated her, and she likes travel and visiting ancient buildings.

**Recent titles by the same author:**

KATHERINE
MASTER OF TAMASEE
HONOUR BOUND

# THE RAINBOROUGH INHERITANCE

## Helen Dickson

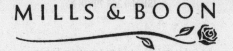

# MILLS & BOON

*MILLS & BOON, the Rose Device and*
*LEGACY OF LOVE are trademarks of the publisher.*
*Harlequin Mills & Boon Limited,*
*Eton House, 18 24 Paradise Road, Richmond, Surrey TW9 1SR*

© Helen Dickson 1996

ISBN 0 263 79878 X

*Set in 11½ on 13 pt Linotron Times*
*04-9611-64404*

*Typeset in Great Britain by CentraCet, Cambridge*
*Printed and bound in Great Britain*
*by BPC Paperbacks Limited, Aylesbury*

# CHAPTER ONE

LAURENCE DWYER walked with purpose in the direction of Lincoln's Inn with his head bowed slightly in brooding preoccupation. He was a strikingly handsome man, an army officer just back from the Mediterranean and the warm Spanish sun, in his late twenties, tall and markedly upright in bearing, his features dark and lean, making claim to good looks and aristocratic distinction, a likely candidate indeed— albeit a reluctant one—to fill the role of the next Earl of Rainborough, heir to the vast Rainborough estate and castle, twenty miles northeast of the ancient city of York, where the town of Rainborough nestled, comfortable and full of charm, surrounded by the wide beautiful vistas of the bracken-clad Yorkshire moors, which in August became a sea of purple heather.

Laurence emerged from an alleyway into a pleasant cobbled courtyard and went directly towards the offices of Gareth and Shard, the lawyers who handled all the affairs of the Dwyer family. He was ushered inside by one of the clerks and, a few moments later, into the office of Mr Shard, the sole occupant, busily writing at his desk. Recognising his visitor immediately Mr Shard, a tall lanky man with blunt features, placed his quill into the inkwell and rose.

'Welcome, my lord!' he exclaimed. 'How good it is to see you—and so soon. In truth, I did not expect you until next week at the earliest. You had a good journey from Spain, I hope?'

'Yes—thank you. Once I received your letter I saw no reason to delay. I took leave of absence from my regiment but I know it is only a matter of time before I must resign my commission.'

Seating himself across the ledger-strewn desk from Mr Shard, Laurence regarded the lawyer seriously, one long-booted leg crossed over the other.

'Yes, of course. You were close to your cousin, I understand. His death must have come as quite a shock.'

'Yes. Rupert and I spent many happy hours together as boys. Due to my commitments with my regiment, I have not seen him for some considerable time—four years, in fact—but nevertheless I shall miss him sorely. I was not aware that he suffered from ill health. What was wrong with him?'

'His death was quite sudden. Sadly, the lure of St James's and the gaming tables was too strong for your cousin to resist. After his father died, with no one to advise him and restrict his spending—although it must be said that both Mr Gareth and myself went to great pains to do just that—alas to no avail—he took to spending a good deal of his time here. From what I understand he contracted a fever prevalent in London at that time and died soon afterwards.'

Laurence nodded, saddened to learn that his cousin had come to so tragic an end. A man of great charm, Rupert had no ambition whatsoever, unlike himself, and his father, unwilling to allow his only son and heir to take a commission in the army, fearing that he would be killed in action, had insisted that he remain at Rainborough and learn how to run the estate. Rupert had raised no objection and had been content to do just that.

Laurence sighed deeply. 'I never thought I would inherit Rainborough and, in truth, Mr Shard, I never had any desire to. Rupert was always so robust. I believed his future was secure—that he would wed the Lady Anne Waddington from over Pickering way whom he was forever hankering after, and that together they would raise a profusion of healthy children.'

Mr Shard nodded with understanding. He had known Laurence Dwyer since he was a boy, when he had come to London with his father,

and later, after his death, with his uncle, the
then Earl of Rainborough. Even then he had
burned with ambition. Once he had got his
commission, he had entered the Foot Guards as
a young subaltern, volunteering for all the
dangerous tasks, and had been complimented
on his exploits which had not gone unnoticed
or unrewarded. He was a soldier of outstanding
ability, having distinguished himself in various
campaigns abroad—at Blenheim, in the
Netherlands and later in Spain, having learnt
his trade with the most celebrated of England's
masters, the Duke of Marlborough. Having
reached the rank of colonel, Laurence Dwyer
was utterly devoted to his regiment. Who could
blame him for not wanting to leave?

'I dare say you will miss the army.'

'Aye. Life with the army was the one I chose.
It suited me well. It will be strange adjusting to
life outside the regiment.'

'I can understand that—but as you know you
are the last of the Dwyers. I cannot say that I
would blame you should you decide to remain
with the army—but, should you not wish to
accept your inheritance, then the entire estate
must be sold.'

Laurence looked at him sharply. 'No, Mr
Shard. That is quite out of the question.'

Mr Shard sighed, shaking his head slowly.
'That is what I expected you to say, but you

may change your mind when you discover its sorry state.'

Laurence's eyes narrowed. 'What are you saying?'

'That owing to your cousin's waywardness—and the land tax, which in itself has proved crippling to many noble families, especially to those not having recovered from sequestrations imposed on them during and after the Civil War—you have inherited a considerable pile of debts. The whole estate has been sadly neglected. To avoid shutting up the castle and selling land, a great deal of money must be acquired—and quickly. I take it that you have no means of your own?'

Laurence shook his head. 'Only what I receive from the army and a small inheritance left me by my father—which is nowhere near the figure I suspect you are speaking of. But something must be done. Rainborough Castle has been the home of the Dwyers for generations. We fought for it and we survived the perilous years of the Civil War. To sell it all is unthinkable.'

'Then—might I put forward a suggestion?' said Mr Shard cautiously.

'Of course—anything—if it will help. What is it you wish to say?'

Not being one to beat about the bush, Mr

Shard came straight to the point. 'That you marry an heiress.'

Laurence scowled, experiencing a sudden surge of anger. Mr Shard and Mr Gareth had clearly discussed this matter together and no doubt had just such an heiress in mind. 'Marriage? No, Mr Shard. I would be grateful if you would kindly refrain from interfering in something which I consider to be an entirely private and personal matter. When I marry, I will choose my own wife.'

Undeterred, for he was certain that what he had suggested was the only solution to the problem, Mr Shard continued. 'I apologise, my lord. Please believe me when I say I meant no offence. Perhaps I put my suggestion clumsily. But please hear what I have to say before you dismiss it completely. You see—I have already been approached by Sir Thomas Howard, who has suggested that you might consider marriage to his daughter. Do you remember the Howard family? They are from your part of the world.'

Yes, Laurence did remember them. The Howards' land bordered the Rainborough estate—although the Howards' acreage was nowhere near as vast. But Thomas Howard was the son of Matthew, who had emigrated to Barbados during the Commonwealth back in 1655—like many other Royalists unwilling to submit to the powers that were at that time.

He remembered his uncle telling him how the Howard estate had suffered more than most as a result of the Civil War and that Matthew, the youngest of Lord Howard's three sons, filled with discontent and unable to see any future for himself in England, had taken his wife and son, Thomas, to Barbados. His father, a hard man, certain that his son was bent on destroying himself, had told him there would be no consideration in his will. Despite this, Matthew had gone to Barbados and, through hard endeavour, had managed to make his way by growing sugar.

'I was under the impression that Sir Thomas was in Barbados?'

'That was the case, but he always had a yearning for England. When his wife died, leaving him with two young daughters, and with himself in failing health, having already made a fortune out of growing sugar, he sold his plantation and brought them to England several months ago, taking up residence with his spinster cousin at Burntwood Hall. Sir Thomas was saddened to learn of the death of your uncle, whom he had met on several occasions during his visits to England over the years, because your family has close ties to the Howards having fought side by side throughout the years of Civil War.'

'But why did he not put his proposition to Rupert?'

'Rupert's dissolute behaviour did not endear him to Sir Thomas—whereas you are a different matter entirely. Your reputation and ability as a soldier and a gentleman are well known. Aware of the debts Rupert had incurred, and the problems that would beset you on your arrival at Rainborough, he came to see me with an eye to marriage between yourself and his eldest daughter. He is afraid that when he is dead Henrietta, who is twenty-one-years old and will be an immensely rich young woman— as will Lucinda, who is just one year younger than her sister—will be beseiged by fortune hunters. It could prove to be disastrous for them with no one to guide them.'

'But what of her younger sister and this cousin of her father's you say she lives with?'

'A husband is also to be found for Lucinda but, alas, Sir Thomas's cousin is too old and ill herself to be of help. It is his dearest wish to see both his daughters settled before his demise—which, by all accounts, could happen at any time. Sir Thomas is a very ill man so you can understand his haste in trying to arrange matters. It would be advantageous to both families if a marriage took place, uniting the Dwyers and the Howards. In fact, with the sad state of the Rainborough estate nothing could be more appropriate. You would gain enormously from the marriage while Miss Howard would gain the title of Countess and the security of marriage.'

Laurence listened to what Mr Shard had to say and as he did so his words were a harsh reminder of his position. Gradually he began to see the sense of his words and he had a sudden vision of his uncle and his father, of their proud and noble bearings and of the long line of his forebears who had suffered to preserve intact the honour and noble name of Dwyer, who had subdued their own lives and fought their own individual battles for that same sense of honour—some making that ultimate sacrifice. Laurence knew he owed it to them to see that Rainborough was made secure for future generations; if he were to sell everything, then surely the Dwyer ghosts would be justified in rising up in anger at his dishonourable deed.

In that moment he could see no alternative to Mr Shard's suggestion—however much he was against it. Besides, there was another matter to be considered other than his inheritance, one which Mr Shard knew nothing about—a matter which made it extremely difficult—if not impossible—for him to return to Spain and his regiment.

Laurence sighed deeply, his expression grim as he faced Mr Shard. 'Very well,' he said firmly. 'You are right, of course. If things are as bad as you say then there really is no alternative. But, before I agree to anything, let it be understood that I must first see for myself the extent of neglect at Rainborough before I commit myself to Miss Howard.'

'As you wish. Miss Howard is herself in London with her father at this time. Would you like me to arrange a meeting?'

'Yes—very well. However—it must be in the next day or so for I must leave for Rainborough as soon as possible.'

Almost two weeks later, seated in the sitting-room of the George Inn in York, along Coney Street, a large establishment where many visitors and people of note lodged when in the city, Lucinda Howard kept glancing towards the door, impatient for her maid to reappear. She had sent her up to her chamber to fetch her bonnet and gloves, having decided to go out into the city to take in the shops in the Minster yard and Pavement.

Confound the girl, she fumed impatiently, annoyed at being kept waiting, although, she sighed, she must try not to be too hard on her; no doubt her services had been commandeered by her aunt who was by no means young and in ill health, and who found it difficult to get about with ease. From the window which faced the street she had been watching passengers alight from a coach which had just arrived from

London across at the busy coaching inn, the Black Swan, with servants running about in a frenzy in order to attend to the newly arrived guests.

The activity over, no longer distracted and unable to wait any longer, Lucinda rose to go in search of her maid, hurriedly climbing the stairs. On the upper landing her attention was caught by a foreign-looking woman holding a child, a little girl, in her arms. Lucinda was momentarily diverted from her quest by the woman's looks which caught her attention, her inky black hair and heavy features and large hooded black eyes which bespoke of Italian or Spanish blood. A rush of emotion and nostalgia swamped her, for she had seen many such women on her island home of Barbados, the island she had never wanted to leave. She was so terribly homesick and thought of it with yearning, of its warmth, its blue sea and skies, which this cold and dismal country could never replace in her heart. She saw that the child, who she assumed must be the woman's daughter, resembled her with her lustrous black curls struggling to be free of the white frilled bonnet, but in contrast her features were fine, her face small and exquisite with long silky lashes fanning her cheeks.

Lucinda was about to pass her by when she noticed with alarm how flushed the woman was and how she swayed slightly. Immediately she moved towards her, afraid lest she fell with the child in her arms.

'Please—let me take the child. You are not well.'

Quickly Lucinda took the child from her. The woman tried to hold on to her, and it seemed to be with some reluctance that she had to let her go.

'I—I am so sorree,' she breathed in faltering English, passing a hand over her brow. 'I—I feel quite faint. It ees coming in here—it ees so hot—so many people—but I have a chamber to go to so please give me back the child.'

Balancing the little girl on one arm Lucinda placed her free hand on the woman's elbow, guiding her along the landing.

'Then let me help you to your chamber. Perhaps you will feel better after lying down.' Lucinda smiled down reassuringly at the child in her arms and the child smiled back. 'What a beautiful child.'

'Yes—yes, she ees. Thank you. You are very kind—but I will be all right now. Come—give me the child,' she requested firmly, holding out her arms.

'No—'

'Please—I can find my own way—truly I can.'

'I will help you,' Lucinda insisted, proceeding along the landing but she was halted suddenly—

'You heard the lady,' said a deep masculine voice brusquely from behind, so close she could almost feel his hot breath on her neck. 'I suggest you do as she says.'

Still holding the child, Lucinda spun round, having to tilt her head back slightly to look up at the man who had come up behind her, with another man following close on his heels carrying some heavy-looking leather bags, which indicated they must have arrived on the London coach, but preferred to stay at the George Inn rather than the Black Swan.

When her eyes locked on his she was quite unprepared for the effect he had on her—her pulses seemed to leap and she found it difficult to compose herself. She gaped up at him; with his deepset green-brown eyes and his rich dark brown hair tied back in the nape of his neck, he was by far the most attractive man she had ever seen in her life. He had the same swarthy dark tan as the men on Barbados who worked their plantations regardless of the sun burning them almost as nut brown as their slaves from Africa. His dark eyebrows were drawn into a scowl across his nose. Never had she seen eyebrows so wicked. Blood rushed to her cheeks for she was suddenly aware that she was staring at him, but the expression in his eyes was so compelling that she was unable to lower her gaze.

'Is there a problem?' he asked, glancing from

one to the other. His face was expressionless but in his narrowed eyes was a spark, grim and formidable, which seemed to say that he wanted no fuss.

Lucinda noticed a shutter come down over the woman's face and that she lowered her gaze to avoid her own. 'Yes. This lady is clearly unwell and needs to lie down,' Lucinda said, surprised at hearing her voice sound normal. 'I was afraid she might fall with the child and injure her.'

'Then give her to me,' said the gentleman, reaching out and taking the child from her, who did not object in the slightest—in fact she seemed quite happy to be held in his arms.

Again Lucinda glanced towards the woman with some concern. 'Perhaps a doctor or an apothecary should be called for?'

'No, that is not necessary. Pray do not concern yourself,' said the gentleman with a small degree of irritability at her persistence, yet he could not prevent his eyes from lingering on her face. There was no denying that this young woman was indeed a beauty, with well-chiselled features and a mass of fashionably arranged fair-coloured hair. Her skin was translucent, her wide eyes the colour of violets and her full, firm lips betrayed a hidden sensuality and strength of purpose. At any other time he would have been more than happy to make her acquaintance but not now.

Lucinda's anger rose and her cheeks flamed. In spite of his good looks she sensed something purposeful and menacing about him, and his slender brown hands, which emerged from fine lace cuffs, and had taken the child from her, made her suspect that if the situation demanded they could be as hard as steel. In her view his behaviour was thoroughly ungrateful, for her intervention might have prevented the woman—probably his wife—from falling and injuring herself and the child. She noticed the woman's nervousness, that this man's presence seemed to increase her agitation, and she kept her eyes lowered, as if she were almost too afraid to look at him. Was she afraid of him? And if so, why?

Lucinda deliberately turned away from the gentleman, directing all her attention to the woman, resenting his easy dismissal of her ill health.

'Would you like me to stay with you until you are recovered?' she asked softly.

She saw the woman's eyes dart to her companion before she shook her head vigorously.

'No—thank you—no.'

'That will not be necessary,' the man intervened sharply. 'I shall see that she is made comfortable myself.'

Lucinda was genuinely angry now and when she turned accusingly the gentleman saw it and, fearing she was about to make a scene, sensed he'd better change his tactics and smiled a reassuring smile, looking down at her with those magnificent green-brown eyes.

'There's absolutely nothing to worry about,' he said, speaking in a persuasive voice. 'We have just arrived on the coach from London. Four days is a long time to be on the road for anyone but with a child it seems interminable. If you have ever travelled some distance in one of those contraptions then you will know there is little comfort in them. I can assure you there was little ease for any of us.'

'By the lady's condition it seems she had less,' commented Lucinda acidly.

'The lady has had a long and arduous journey. I'm sure that after resting and some refreshment she will feel a good deal better. Is that not so, Maria?'

Maria nodded, smiling gratefully at Lucinda who suspected the smile was forced to satisfy the gentleman. She stepped back, realising that further protestations would be both foolish and counter-productive.

'In that case there is nothing more to be said.'

'No—nothing at all,' the gentleman replied coldly, 'and I would be obliged if you would step aside to let us pass.'

Realising that she was being dismissed and was also blocking their path, Lucinda stepped aside. Well, she thought—handsome this man might be but that was the only thing to his credit. She considered him to be unmannerly, exceedingly rude, a bully and a brute. May God help the poor woman if she had the misfortune to be his wife.

'Very well. I bid you good day.'

The gentleman merely bowed his head in assent and watched as Lucinda turned and disappeared inside her own chamber before taking the woman's elbow and propelling her along the landing.

Unbeknown to Lucinda, who had closed the door to her chamber and was leaning on it breathlessly, she had just made the acquaintance of Laurence Dwyer, the Earl of Rainborough, unaware of who he was and how important he was to be to her future. Just then she did not suppose she would ever see him again. But, brute and bully though he might be, one thing was certain—she would not forget him in a hurry.

Lucinda considered York to be a pleasant and beautiful city, with its wide, navigable river and quaint, tightly packed streets, flanked by buildings with jettied roofs and timbered gables, some streets so narrow they would hardly take the width of a coach. Every other place was a gate or a bar which she found so confusing. She was in York to do some shopping with her Aunt Celia, who had long since promised her this visit to the ancient city. With Lucinda's sister Henrietta away in London with their father, it had seemed the perfect opportunity, but Celia did not enjoy good health, and today was one of her bad days so she remained in her room resting while Lucinda went out into the city accompanied by her maid, Nancy.

Celia was their father's cousin but because she remained their closest living relative it had long since been agreed that she should be known to Henrietta and Lucinda as Aunt Celia.

Together Lucinda and Nancy negotiated the intricate tangle of streets enclosed within the limestone ribbon of wall, proceeding to walk along Stonegate towards the Minster yard where they admired the fine large houses situated around the Minster, especially the Deanery, a building of many notable events during the Civil War, when King Charles I had been in York and he had convened a Great Council here of the Peers of the Realm.

In the Minster yard they browsed in a bookseller's and a draper's, with fancy silks, rich brocades and striped mantuas. They bought some perfumed comfits and macaroons from a confectioner before moving on along Petergate because Lucinda wanted to look at the markets, being careful to avoid the Shambles where the air was thick with bluebottles. It was a smelly, obnoxious street where butchers set up their flesh benches in the open air. They walked towards Thursday Market to view its splendid new market cross, a hall which was supported on five open arches topped by a turret and a weather vane. It provided a shelter below and a room where plays were performed above.

They strolled along the street towards Pavement, where All Saints Church stood with its graceful octagonal lantern tower. Her Aunt Celia had told her that in medieval times a large lamp was hung there, lit at night to act as a beacon for travellers to aim at who were making their way to York through the dense Forest of Galtres to the north of the city. They passed a butter factor and chandler, smelling the pleasant aroma of Jamaica rums, French and British brandies and cinnamon waters, stopping to browse in a shop which sold an elegant assortment of perfume and essence pots, snuff boxes and ivory toys from London and Germany.

Having purchased some trinkets, they made their way slowly down High Ousegate and back along Coney Street towards the George Inn.

They were just about to pass the gateway which led into the inn yard when, at that moment, a horseman came clattering out over the cobblestones with such haste—evidently in a hurry to reach his destination—that to avoid being trampled underfoot Lucinda, with a cry, stepped back quickly, stumbling in the process and falling painfully to the ground, scattering her packages about her in the dirt. Nancy rushed to her in alarm, kneeling beside her.

Seeing the sudden movement out of the corner of his eye, the horseman pulled his mount to a halt and, turning in the saddle, looked back. Upon seeing Lucinda on the ground, he immediately dismounted and strode over to her.

Raising her head, her body feeling bruised and sore, Lucinda saw the horseman looming over her and recognised him immediately as being that insufferable man she had met on the landing earlier. He reached out a strong brown hand and, seizing her arm, helped her to her feet. Putting her weight on her left foot, she suddenly winced with pain.

'Are you hurt?' he demanded. 'I saw you trip.'

Lucinda stared at him incredulously, her eyes sparking with anger. 'Trip? I did not trip. Why—had I not thrown myself out of the way of your mount I would have been trampled on. You came riding out of the inn yard as if the devil himself were after you.'

'Then if that is so I apologise. I did not see you there.'

'Evidently,' she snapped, pulling her arm free from his grasp and supporting herself with one hand on the wall while brushing at the dirt on her skirts with the other. Gingerly she put a little weight on her injured foot, almost crying out at the pain that shot through it. It was beginning to throb terribly.

'Your ankle is hurt,' he said sternly. 'Here— let me help you.'

'No,' said Lucinda quickly as he reached out his hand, looking at Nancy who was picking the dropped packages up off the ground. 'I'll manage perfectly well with Nancy to help me. It is only a sprain. I don't need your help.'

Laurence scowled at her, noticing the stubborn thrust to her chin which told him she would rather die than accept his help, but her eyes were swimming with the silently repressed tears that the pain from her injured ankle was causing. It was evident that she would not make it up to her room unaided. His eyes narrowed.

'I doubt that. Come—don't be difficult,' he said impatiently. 'I am in a hurry and enough time has been wasted as it is.'

Before Lucinda could stop him or protest, he had placed one arm firmly about her waist and the other beneath her knees, swinging her effortlessly up into his arms. Normally she would have kicked and fought at being handled in such a way, but she was too stunned to say anything at finding herself pressed so close to him. She could feel his warmth and the strength in his hard lean body, which made her feel uncomfortable—and something else as well, which she could not identify.

After they had reached her room and Laurence had placed her on a chair, he dropped on one knee and removed her shoe, flexing her ankle with the professional expertise of a doctor. Lucinda could feel the firmness of his fingers through her stocking; as he twisted her foot to one side, she gripped the arms of the chair, almost crying out with the pain this caused her, but bit her lip in her determination not to let him know how much it hurt. At last he put her foot gently on the carpet and looked up at her directly.

'You were right. There's nothing broken— just a slight sprain. Get your maid to bind your ankle firmly and rest it. You'll be walking on it in a few days.'

'Why—*thank you*, doctor,' she said with emphasis.

Ignoring her sarcastic tone Laurence's lips curled in a wry smile. 'I'm not a doctor,' he confided. 'I'm a soldier and used to dealing with broken bones and the like—although I have to say that none of the soldiers under my com-

mand have quite so charming an ankle.' He
stood up, looking down at her upturned face
which had flushed slightly in embarrassment at
his remark. His dark eyes twinkled. 'I assure
you, you will be all right—and I apologise if,
because of my recklessness, I have ruined your
visit to York. You are visiting?'

'Yes,' she retorted, 'and yes, you have ruined
it. I am here with my aunt and now, it seems,
we shall have to return home earlier than we
intended.'

'You are right to reproach me. If I could
repair the damage then believe me, I would,' he
said softly.

Lucinda fixed him with an unblinking gaze.
On seeing that he did indeed look genuinely
sorry her manner melted towards him a little,
and when she next spoke her tone was kinder.

'Yes, I'm sure you would. However, it was
just an accident—' she relented '—and I did not
mean to reproach you. You said you were in a
hurry. Please do not let me detain you any
longer.'

Alone, Lucinda reflected on her meeting with
the stranger and was curious as to his identity.
He had a powerful physical presence which had
seemed to fill the whole room and, despite
being the cause of her sprained ankle, his
behaviour towards her had been perfectly cour-

teous. On reflection, she remembered seeing how thick his hair was when he had bent his head to examine her foot, how broad his shoulders were and, when he had looked at her, how taut his skin was stretched over his cheekbones, and how frank and interesting had been his gaze when he had fixed his deep brown eyes, flecked with green, on hers.

He had told her he was a soldier—which explained his tanned face and hands, indicating that he'd seen service abroad. Giving herself up to Nancy's ministerings as she bound her foot, she sighed, experiencing a feeling of regret that she would never see him again.

Meanwhile, as Laurence made his way back down to the street, he was feeling the same sense of regret, for he had thought the young woman quite enchanting. There was something so fresh about her; her vibrant personality positively burned in those glorious violet eyes. He was not deceived by her aloof manner, suspecting that, beneath her would-be hardness, there was a fawn-like vulnerability that cried out for his sympathy.

After retrieving his horse he rode along Coney Street, unable to resist the impulse of stopping to purchase a bunch of red and white sweet-scented roses from a flower seller. Slipping a coin into the palm of an eager young boy, he asked him to deliver them to the

George Inn to a certain young lady with a
sprained ankle, giving him clear instructions as
to which room she occupied, before riding out
of York alone towards the north-east, in the
direction of Rainborough.

# CHAPTER TWO

Two weeks after her return from York, when
Lucinda's father and Henrietta returned from
London, she saw with some concern that all was
not well with her sister. She noticed how pale
she was—in fact, she had never seen her so
pale, but it was not until they were alone in
Lucinda's room that she discovered how deeply
upset and disturbed she was by her visit to
London.

Henrietta had known before she left Howard
Lodge the purpose of her father's visit, that he
intended calling on the Earl of Rainborough's
lawyers with the purpose of proposing a match
between the Earl and his daughter. But
Henrietta's head was so in the clouds over her
love for Hal Ingram, a squire's son from the
next village of Carthwait, that in her bewildered
young mind she had truly thought her father
would not go ahead with what he intended
when he saw how averse she was to the match.

But her father was resolved to finding suitable husbands for both his daughters before his
demise. He had been careful to conceal from
either of them just how ill he was from the

growth that was slowly growing and eating away at his insides. But Lucinda, with her sharp, observant eyes, missed nothing, so she was not insensible to his discomfort, but she had no idea and would have been deeply shocked to know just how serious it was.

'Oh, Lucinda, what is to be done?' said Henrietta with an urge to confide in someone at last.

'Done? Why—what do you speak of, Henrietta?'

'This—this marriage to the Earl of Rainborough. I cannot go through with it, Lucinda. I simply cannot.'

'But I understood the Earl to be in favour of Father's proposition.'

Unbidden tears came suddenly to Henrietta's eyes but she blinked them away. 'I know. And how happy Father would be if I were in agreement. How it would please him—but I cannot.'

'Why? Because of Hal?'

Henrietta nodded. 'I cannot think of a life without Hal. I cannot live without him,' she groaned despairingly.

Never had Lucinda seen her sister in such a state. Alarmed by this, she went over to Henrietta at once, feeling a great need to protect her, taking her hands and drawing her down beside her onto a low divan.

'Have you spoken to Father? Have you told him how you feel about Hal?'

Henrietta nodded. 'Yes—but he will not listen. Every time I mention his name, he retreats into himself. When I first met Hal and we fell in love, everything seemed so simple. I planned it all in my mind—that we would become betrothed and then married. How was I to know that Father would take against his family so? I know his father's reputation for the gaming tables and his love of strong liquor discredits him in Father's eyes—and that his older brothers are little better—but Hal is not like them. He is kind. He loves me and cares not one jot about Father's money. He says he would marry me if I had nothing at all.'

Lucinda did not contradict her. Hal Ingram's adoration and the gallantry he showed towards Henrietta were plain to all when they were together—which was not often, for their father had done his utmost to discourage the relationship.

'Tell me what happened between you and the Earl of Rainborough? What he's like?'

'Nothing—nothing at all happened. We met after he and Father had had a long discussion— that is all. He is undeniably handsome and charming; in fact, any woman would be honoured to marry such a man. I am certain there is not a woman in the whole of England who—

having met him—would not die for a rendez-vous with him. His lineage is impeccable, he has distinguished himself in countless battles all over Europe and is highly thought of by the Duke of Marlborough himself. . .'

'But?'

Henrietta fixed imploring eyes on hers. 'Oh, Lucinda—in truth he is so excessively male and formidable. He radiates a force and vitality that scares me half to death. The mere prospect of marriage to him terrifies me.' She sighed deeply, lowering her eyes and looking down at her hands folded quietly in her lap. 'How fool-ish you must think me, you, who have never been afraid of anything or anyone in your entire life.'

Lucinda sighed, for Henrietta spoke the truth. The two of them were alike in colouring, yet in temperament they were so very different. Whereas Lucinda was self-willed, lively and restless, full of energies she found difficult to repress, with nothing of Henrietta's unselfish forbearing, Henrietta was of a more simple, timid nature, the epitome of placid indolence, often overcome with shyness and sudden blushes when in the company of the opposite sex and, Lucinda thought, if the Earl of Rainborough was as strong and formidable in character as her sister would have her believe, then she would have been more timid and embarrassed than usual, for such men never failed to discompose her.

Henrietta was not as tall as Lucinda. Her eyes were a limpid blue, whereas Lucinda's were a deep shade of violet which became lighter or darker depending on her mood. They had always been close.

'Father is hoping that matters will proceed to a satisfactory conclusion,' Henrietta went on, 'and I know I should feel honoured—and I am—but I would give all my prospects to anyone who would take them from me—simply to marry Hal. Good, simple, ordinary Hal. Oh—he isn't rich or anything like that, but then, neither is the Earl.'

'Not now, perhaps, but marriage to you would change all that,' retorted Lucinda coldly, feeling some resentment towards the Earl of Rainborough. She did not blame her father for wanting the best for Henrietta, but what manner of man was it that would take a wife merely to pay off his debts incurred by his cousin and to repair the neglect on his estate? And who was to know that he wouldn't do the same as his erstwhile cousin anyway and squander his new-found fortune, as seemed to be common among most of the English aristocracy? She could feel nothing but contempt for any man who would marry a woman for the size of her dowry rather than herself, and there was

no doubt in her mind that the Earl of
Rainborough would jump at the chance of
marrying Henrietta.

Lucinda sighed, trying to think of something
comforting to say that would alleviate her sister's fears. 'Father is only doing what he consid-
ers is best, Henrietta. I'm sure he wouldn't want
you to be unhappy. You worry yourself to no
purpose.'

'I do so hope you're right. You understand,
don't you, Lucinda? I have no love to give
anyone but Hal. The Earl is important, that I
know. He owns a vast estate and castle and if I
married him I would become a countess—but
that means nothing to me. I cannot marry
merely for gain and position. It is not what I
want. I must have love above all else. You must
understand that. Do you think that is selfish of
me?'

'No.' Lucinda smiled. 'How can I when I
want the same things myself? But more than
anything else,' she said wistfully, a faraway
expression in her eyes, 'I want to return to
Barbados. Every night I go to bed I pray that
when I wake up I shall be back in my bed at
Lynton, with Deborah bringing me my hot
chocolate and pulling back the drapes—flooding my room with brilliant sunlight—and I
would smell the newly turned earth in the fields
and the hibiscus and bougainvillaea clinging to

the veranda beneath my window, and hear the chanting of the negroes working in the fields. Oh, Henrietta—it's all so far away from us now. The very thought of never going back, never seeing it again, breaks my heart.'

'I know—and I too wanted to return to all that until I met Hal. But now I am content to be where ever he is. One day it will be the same for you, Lucinda. You'll see. You're so lucky not to be in the same predicament as myself.'

'Not so lucky. Remember it is to be my turn next. Father is set upon finding both of us a husband with considerable haste, it seems.'

'I know, but I doubt it will be the sort of match he is preparing for me. Why does he have to aim so high?'

'Because of the fortune we will inherit, Henrietta, and owing to the fact that we have no immediate family—only Aunt Celia, whose health, as you know, gives us all cause for concern—I suspect he wants to make quite sure we are settled and everything is taken care of before—before. . .'

Something in her faltering tone caused Henrietta to look at her sharply. 'Before? Before what, Lucinda? Do you think Father is very ill? Is that what you are trying to say?'

'I don't know, but there is no denying that he has lost some of his toughness and vigour. There is a frailty about him and there are times when he appears to suffer a great deal of discomfort. He also tires so easily. However, you must tell him how you feel, Henrietta. You must find some way of making him see that you love Hal—that you cannot marry the Earl of Rainborough. And if the man is so desperate to retain his estate and castle, then he must look elsewhere for some other heiress to marry.'

The sun blazed down on the annual Rainborough fair held in the surrounding fields of Rainborough town. It had the promise of being a glittering and rowdy affair. People came from far and wide dressed in their finest apparel—farmers and esquires, their wives and daughters—filling every road and track for miles around. Gipsies, with their colourful caravans and strings of ponies and horses, all travelled in the direction of Rainborough fair, where open stalls under brightly coloured awnings had been erected and where all manner of merchandise was sold.

Delicious smells of various foods cooking on stalls had been set out like small banquets—mouthwatering roast pork, roast goose, gingerbread and gooseberry pie. Great crowds were attracted to the waxwork booths and freak shows, which Lucinda avoided, wondering how people could be so ghoulishly fascinated by dwarfs and deformities.

Here the not so well-to-do rubbed shoulders with the better off. Usually it was the fashionable thing for the sophisticated townspeople, with their perfume and pomades, to despise the common country folk, stinking of their animals and fields, but for these two days of the fair they flocked in their hundreds in their fancy carriages, driven by dandified footmen, to see the booths and curiosities displayed and would dally to partake of the dancing and merrymaking which went on long after dark.

It was the first fair Lucinda had ever been to in her life; there was nothing like this on Barbados. She had wanted Henrietta to accompany her but her sister had managed to escape the watchful eye of her father to keep a secret assignation with Hal instead, so she had to be content with Nancy. She sauntered aimlessly between the stalls followed by Nancy, pushing her way through the noisy crowd, avoiding the crude prize fights, unwilling to look upon bloody noses and burst lips, preferring instead the novelty of the puppet shows, the jugglers and acrobats.

When she passed the bright purple-and-gold coloured gipsy fortune teller's tent, she contemplated whether or not to go in and have her palm read but decided against it. There was only one thing the gypsy could tell her that would make her happy and that was for her to return to Barbados, to Lynton, the house in which she had lived all her life until coming to England, but she knew that was the one thing she would not be told.

But at the thought of her beloved Barbados sudden pain wrung her heart and hot tears stung her lids. One day she would return, she promised herself fiercely. She had to. Not even the kind of love Henrietta felt for Hal Ingram would make the memory of her island home fade.

She paused to toss some wooden hoops onto pegs, failing to win the adorable little painted doll, and she sipped a mug of lemonade beneath the shade of a tree, when she suddenly realised that Nancy had wandered away from her side. Annoyed by this, Lucinda began searching for her, eventually drawn towards a crowd gathered outside one of the large tents where mugs of ale were being sold and where music was playing loudly and dancers stomped around on the grass to the merry rhythm. Looking through a break in the crowd, she craned her neck to see what was causing so much interest and amusement. She soon saw what it was. Her heart plummeted when she recognised Nancy's cherry red dress and realised that she was the centre of everyone's attention.

Men in smocks slouched against barrels, unashamedly slaking their voracious appetites for ale, determined to make the most of these two days of idleness, for the fair days were the only high days and holidays of their year. Doubtless many would be too drunk by nightfall to find their way home without the aid of a horse and cart.

The air was rent with coarse laughter and lewd remarks, the crowd yelling with a great deal of delight and a slapping of thighs, shouting encouragement to a burly man, whose wide lips were curled into a leering grin as he harassed Nancy, a pretty young girl with full rounded breasts and a saucy expression, which frequently made her the target of masculine attention. The swaying man had his arm about her waist as he tried to ply her with ale from a foaming mug, clumsily slopping some down her bodice.

'Come, my pretty one,' he slurred. 'Come on and have a drink.'

Emitting a little squeal, Nancy responded by turning her head away, a movement which made her long auburn curls dance wildly, causing the crowd to roar with laughter.

Unable to stand by and watch her maid being made a spectacle of, without a moment's hesitation Lucinda angrily began pushing her way through the crowd towards Nancy, who did not appear to be enjoying the attention—but neither was she resisting very hard, which angered Lucinda further. She did not see Laurence Dwyer lounging lazily against a tree to one side of the tent, absently watching the entertainment with some amusement and trying to remember where he had seen the saucy young wench before.

Upon seeing Lucinda emerge from the crowd in a striking billowing white dress with a bright blue sash, he became lost in fascination, transfixed by the scene. Her limbs propelled her across the grass with lightning speed and immediately she held centre stage. She was swift and supple, with the long limbs of a young colt and fleecy light golden hair.

Somewhere in his mind a bell of recognition rang and almost at once he recalled where he had seen her before, which caused his lips to curve in a slow smile and his eyes to dance with merciless merriment; as he continued his observation of her, his interest deepened.

Lucinda's eyes blazed with so much anger that the man still holding Nancy stepped back a pace.

'Let go her,' she fumed, reaching out and pulling Nancy from his crude embrace.

The man's eyes opened wide in amazement, but then he lurched forward, realising that here was an even greater prize. 'Now—don't be so upperty, miss. Come and have a drink with old Jake. You'll find me accommodating and more than obliging. I know how to give a little lady as pretty as you a good time.'

Lucinda looked at him coldly. 'You're drunk and you're also disgusting,' she snapped and, as the man lurched towards her with his hands outstretched, quite unafraid of his towering bulk she gave him a shove which sent him sprawling to the ground, at which an uproarious cheer went up from the spectators.

Lucinda reached out and snatched an amazed Nancy's wrist; turning on her heel, she pulled her along after her.

'Come along, Nancy,' she scolded, 'and don't you dare stray from my side again.'

In a few seconds they had reached the edge of the crowd where Lucinda paused and looked at her maid.

'Are you all right?'

Nancy smiled faintly. Her auburn hair had come loose from its pins and her dress was stained and crumpled, but apart from that she showed no visible sign of suffering.

'Yes,' she replied, wiping her perspiring forehead. 'Those louts behaved much the same as other men hereabouts when in drink.'

In spite of her pursed lips, Nancy sounded almost gay and there was a sparkle to her eyes—making Lucinda wonder whether she had not rather enjoyed the experience, for she was well aware that she kept an eye out for handsome young men. Nancy had become her maid when she had first come to live at Burntwood Hall, a large rambling house and the ancestral home of the Howards, on the edge of Rainborough town. At first Lucinda had missed Deborah, her maid back home on Barbados, but she had soon become used to Nancy's ways. She was a simple girl with never a serious thought in her head. Give her a trinket and a tryst with a good-looking young man and she was blissfully happy.

'Come, Nancy, I think it's time we went home. We must find Matthew with the carriage—although it will not be easy in this crowd. Father was reluctant to let us come in the first place and will be so angry if we are late back.'

To find their way out of the fairground to where Matthew would be waiting with the carriage, they had to pass by the front of the tent and Laurence, still leaning against the tree. Lucinda found her eyes drawn by an irresistible urge to the spot where he stood, watching her. She was about to look away but then stopped, speechless, her progress checked by her amazement, for she recognised him immediately and was so surprised at the sight of him that she could not for a moment believe her eyes.

Their eyes met and locked, and, remembering their meeting in York, Lucinda's opened wider and wider, expressing astonishment—

incredulity—but then she recollected herself
and drew herself up sharply, remembering the
distress of the young foreign woman with the
child and this man's indifference, and also the
discomfort of her own sprained ankle caused by
his recklessness. She also remembered the
flowers but thrust the surprise and joy she had
experienced on receiving them to the back of
her mind—that is, if he had been the one who
had sent them to her. Yet she could think of no
one else and the boy who had delivered them
had given her a fair description of him.

That he must have been standing there for
some time, watching Nancy being harassed by
that drunken oaf with some amusement she did
not doubt, being all too well aware of his
indifference towards the suffering of ladies. He
had done nothing to stop her torment, enjoying
the entertainment Nancy had provided as much
as the rest. He was leaning lazily against the
tree, tall and superbly built, wearing black
knee-length boots and tight dove-coloured
breeches, a loosely fitting white lawn shirt
tucked into the waistband of his breeches and
his dark brown hair tied back with a black
ribbon, a rebellious lock blowing gently across
his forehead. Lucinda looked into his sardoni-
cally smiling dark eyes.

'So—fate has decreed that we meet again,'
he said, abandoning his idle stance and coming

to stand before her, bowing politely but without taking his bold appreciative eyes off her and smiling broadly. 'It is a great pleasure to see you once more—and—if I may say so—you are more charming than ever.'

'Please—save your flattery for someone else. I'm not interested—and nor do I believe in fate, sir,' Lucinda replied tartly.

Laurence laughed outright at her reply. 'I see you are recovered from your sprained ankle— if not your temper.'

'Yes—thank you. I am quite recovered—and my temper is as it always is when I'm in such disagreeable company.'

He nodded, chuckling softly, thinking how vibrant she looked with her flashing eyes and flushed cheeks—with the heat of the day or anger he knew not which, but strongly suspected it was the latter.

'I thought I recognised your maid but for the very life of me I could not remember where I had seen her before—but now I do remember,' he said, meeting her cool gaze. His eyes appraised her, but not in the way men's eyes usually appraised her. This man's eyes saw inside her, piercing through her clothes, seeking to find something other than was obvious.

'So—you are a party to this. While you were trying so hard to remember who she was, did it not occur to you to rescue her from her predicament?'

'It seemed to me that the young lady was more than capable of taking care of herself.'

'Then you were mistaken,' Lucinda retorted, finding the faint twinkle of laughter in the depths of his dark eyes infuriating. 'Surely you could not fail to see—as I did myself—that when faced with a crowd of drunken oafs any woman is quite defenceless. I took you for a gentleman, sir, and would have assumed that she would be free from assault with such as yourself looking on.

'However,' she said, squaring her chin and lifting her head imperiously and throwing back her hair, which caught the golden light of the sun, 'when I remember our meeting prior to this—and the young lady who was with you then, obviously in some distress, and of your lack of consideration—then I should have known better than to expect it of you.'

For a second her words caused Laurence's lean face to darken and his mouth to tighten, but he was momentarily distracted from her accusing words by a soft breeze which blew a silken strand of her hair across her face which became caught on her moist lips. He watched as she lifted up a hand and brushed it absently away. Good Lord, he thought, feeling a burning sensation deep in his loins, finding the gesture highly provocative in its simplicity, knowing she would be innocently unaware of just how tantalising it was. Admiration stirred inside him, for it was the first time in years that anyone had dared accuse him of unmannerly conduct.

'Then what can I say?' he said with elaborate gravity. 'In the light of your accusations I stand rebuked. It would seem that I have been away from England with the army for so long that I have forgotten how to behave as a gentleman should. I do promise to mend my ways.'

'Whether you do or not has nothing whatsoever to do with me, sir,' she said, smarting beneath his narrowed gaze of cynical amusement. 'The young woman I saw you with in York is fully recovered, I hope?'

'Perfectly. As I said at the time—it was nothing more than fatigue after so long a journey. After resting, she was fully recovered.'

'Then I am glad to hear it.'

Hearing the discourse between them a man, the one Lucinda had seen in York on the landing at the inn, came to stand by his side. His name was William Fielding and he had faithfully served Laurence throughout his military career, proving to be indispensable. Reluctant to leave his side, William had willingly come to Rainborough to continue to serve him as his valet. There was a slightly shocked

expression in his eyes, for evidently the young
lady had no idea to whom she was speaking.

'My dear young lady,' he said, 'the gentleman
you are addressing is—'

Lucinda cut the man dead with the glance of
a cobra. 'I am all too well aware of what the
gentleman is,' she said acidly.

William would have said more but, with his
eyes gleaming wickedly, Laurence put a
restraining hand on his arm at which he stepped
back.

Still protectively holding Nancy's wrist,
Lucinda turned from them. 'Come along,
Nancy. It is high time we were getting back. I
think you have provided enough entertainment
for these gentlemen for one day—whoever they
may be.'

'Tell me,' said Laurence, reluctant to see her
go, 'did you receive the flowers I sent you by
way of an apology for my recklessness that day
in York—and to cheer you?'

Lucinda halted in her tracks and turned in
sudden confusion, her cheeks flushed at the
memory. She was conscious of a sudden feeling
of embarrassment for she recalled how flattered
she had been to know that he had still been
thinking of her when he'd ridden off. When
their visit to York had been cut short because
of her sprained ankle, she had taken the flowers
back with her to Burntwood Hall, changing the

water in their vase regularly in order to maintain their freshness, and was sad when they had wilted and died—but she would rather die than let him know this.

'Yes—thank you—but there was really no need. I—I was not sure who sent them. There was no note—no way of knowing, you see.'

Laurence eyed her questioningly. 'So—from what you say you imply that there was someone else whom you thought might have sent them. An admirer, perhaps?'

'I never said that,' Lucinda replied coolly, disliking his easy manner and steady gaze which perturbed her. Her temper began to rise again at his audacity. 'But if that was the case then it is entirely my own affair.'

'And doubtless he is more of a gentleman than I,' Laurence remarked with irony, his eyes narrowed with a hint of mockery in their dark depths.

'From my observations where you are concerned, sir, it would be difficult for him to be less. Whatever you may say—and whoever you may be—the proprieties required of a true gentleman do not seem to be your strong point,' Lucinda said hotly, turning from him once again, eager to be on her way.

'What? Not even if I told you that I was the Earl of Rainborough himself?' Laurence laughed with a hint of truth but also in jest, not in the least offended by her heated remark.

'Ha!' scoffed Lucinda, tossing her head in disbelief and striding off across the grass. 'If that is so, then I am the Queen of England. From what I have been told of the Earl of Rainborough he is a gentleman of the highest order. I am sure the two of you are worlds apart,' she threw back at him over her shoulder.

The two men watched them go with an expression of stunned admiration on their faces.

'Whew,' said William. 'That is some lady. If I am not mistaken—isn't she the young woman you encountered in York?'

'Aye—the very same.'

'Then she must be from these parts. She's spirited enough—that's plain. Wonder who she is?'

'I've no idea, William,' Laurence murmured, for the young lady was clearly no milk sop of a miss and he felt a rush of envy for the man whose task it would be to tame her. 'If I were not on the brink of becoming betrothed to Miss Henrietta Howard, then I'd sure as hell find out.'

# CHAPTER THREE

HAVING left the noise of the fair behind, it was late afternoon when Laurence paused beneath the leafy branches of a giant ash and gazed around at his inheritance. From his vantage point the landscape that unfolded before him was mellow and peaceful, the stretches of open moorland to the east broken here and there by clumps of trees and a string of ponds curving along the bottom of a valley.

He looked to the north where the hills rose skyward, their slopes clothed with trees, and further still to the wildness and solitude breathing from the high bare fells where the air was pure. In winter the heavy snow falls turned the land into a white wilderness, which had cost many a man his life, but on summer days it became paradise on earth.

At the bottom of the hill on which he stood he saw the loop of the river where he had once fished and swam as a boy with Rupert. He allowed his gaze to follow its course, like a long sinuous artery threading through and feeding the land, its flow broken by small islands fringed by weeds between steep banks. Here the water

51

was blue, reflecting the sky, but further on it would become grey from the shadow of the castle walls.

He looked back in the direction of Rainborough town, the view around the outlying hamlets one of small fields where moorland had been cleared away, coarse with stubble now the reapers had done their work. His eyes drank their fill, seeming to sooth the ache inside him that the wrench from his regiment had left.

He sighed, letting his mind go back to his years in Spain. After the Battle of Blenheim, which had been a resounding victory for the Duke of Marlborough—an event which had saved central Europe from domination by France—in 1705 he had gone to Spain, where the War of the Spanish Succession had been taking place for three years.

On the death of Carlo II of Spain in 1700, Louis XIV of France had installed a French Bourbon, his grandson, Philip of Anjou, on the Spanish throne. The Spanish had accepted Philip, believing that Spain would be better served by a Bourbon monarch who could count on Louis XIV's support against the main trading nations of Europe and the Colonies. By so doing, Spain was no longer master of her own destiny and had become a theatre of war.

Although Louis XIV had assured Britain that the Crowns of Spain and France would remain separate and that he wished to avoid war, he had sent French troops into the Spanish Netherlands and seized the frontier fortresses, thus threatening Holland's independence. Conflict had become inevitable and England, Holland and Austria had banded together, unable to countenance a Franco-Spanish alliance which would enable France to dominate Europe and the Straits of Gibraltar from Spanish ports like Cadiz and Malaga, which would strangle British and Dutch trade with the Levant.

Laurence went out at a time when Gibraltar had been taken by the English and Dutch fleet, and when the Habsburg claimant to the Spanish throne, King Charles III, had arrived in Spain. Laurence had been based at the garrison at Gibraltar to help defend the rock from the Spanish counter-offensive on land, and had also spent his energies attacking trading towns and trying to deliver Spain from the French on behalf of their rightful King, Charles III.

With a deep feeling of regret he directed his gaze towards Rainborough Castle, his eyes travelling across the low meadowland, now clothed in king cups and giant moon pennies, which the river always flooded after heavy rain. Followed by William he began to ride down the hill, entering the castle grounds through a castellated gateway and riding up a long sweeping drive beneath the shade of giant elms which flanked him on either side.

Rainborough Castle, built in the thirteenth century, was less of a castle and more of a fortified manor house. Although outwardly defensive with its sturdy walls, sufficient to protect its inhabitants from marauding bands in the past, it could never have withstood a sustained attack. Laurence's ancestors, who had been granted the lands and castle of Rainborough during the reign of Queen Elizabeth, had made great changes to the castle over the years, combining strength with comfort, seeing to it that it contained all the requirements for grand and graceful living. Only in recent years had it been allowed to fall into decay.

When the castle rose before him, its windows lit up like a wall of flame as the late afternoon sun caught the many panes, Laurence paused, his mood somewhat despondent and thoughtful, for he was painfully aware of the countless tasks waiting to be done in order to restore the building to its former glory. Since his return he had discovered the full extent of Rainborough's neglect and that Mr Shard had been correct when he had said a great deal of money was needed to put things right. Out of an army of servants once employed at the castle only a few remained, which included the housekeeper and her husband, prepared to work for very little out of loyalty to the Dwyers.

Elevated to authority in the army, Laurence was already accustomed to people coming to him for advice, and as soon as word got around the district of his arrival he was inundated with callers—mainly wanting remuneration for unpaid debts. With his bailiff he rode the length and breadth of the estate, inspecting everything with a keen eye. Nothing escaped his notice. He visited disgruntled tenant farmers, whose roofs needed repairing, whose barns were tumbling down and who pointed out that the bridges across the river were barely safe to cross.

Signs of disrepair were to be seen all over Rainborough; when Laurence had first seen the extent of the neglect for himself, the price he would have to pay to clear the debts and restore the estate weighed heavily upon him. He sighed, sorely tempted to pursue the delightful young woman he had met in York and then again today at the fair, but common sense and hard-headed realism came to the fore, for unless he sold Rainborough then there was urgent need for a wife—a rich wife. For better or worse, this was his home and he must accept the conditions as they were, yet, being the kind of man he was, he vowed to return it to its former state. He turned to William, a determined set to his face.

'I would like you to send word to Burntwood Hall, William. Inform Sir Thomas that I shall be calling on him at a time which is convenient. I think it is high time I became better acquainted with his daughter.'

The impending visit of the Earl of Rainborough to Burntwood Hall plunged the whole household into a turmoil. Celia considered what would be appropriate for both girls to wear for such an important visitor while Henrietta flew into a state of panic; to her the unthinkable was about to happen. In desperation, she made an emotional appeal to her father, begging him to allow her to marry Hal Ingram.

Thomas Howard was not normally a hard man but he was decisive in all things, aloof and authoritarian. He lived by an uncompromising code of rigid moral principles and there was absolutely no way he would allow his daughter to marry a man belonging to a family with such a dissolute reputation.

Because he was always busy with plantation matters on Barbados, Henrietta and Lucinda were not very well acquainted with their father when they were growing up. He was fond of them but had been happy to leave their upbringing to their mother. Only when she had

died had he begun to take a serious interest in
their welfare. In this matter of Henrietta's
future he remained steadfast, telling her that
what one wanted and what one might have
were not always the same thing, and that if the
Earl of Rainborough was agreeable to the
match, then she would marry him and be happy.
It was his wish and he would not be denied this.

After courageously telling her father that she
would not marry the Earl on any account,
Henrietta hadn't dared contradict him further.
Tearfully she had fled to her room, swearing to
Lucinda—who had listened to the angry inter-
change between them, fearful as to her own
fate—that if he insisted on forcing her into
marriage with the fearsome Earl of
Rainborough then she would run away.

Believing this to be nothing more than the
ravings of her lovesick sister, that she would
think more clearly after a good night's sleep,
Lucinda thought little of her outburst just then,
but when the Earl of Rainborough finally
arrived at Burntwood Hall she was soon to
realise that Henrietta had made no idle threat.

The Earl was to arrive during the afternoon,
but when it was almost time Henrietta was
nowhere to be found. She had gone out riding
with a groom earlier. There was nothing
unusual in this as both girls loved to ride, but
when Henrietta failed to return in time for the

Earl's visit panic set in and servants were dispatched with haste to find her.

In an effort to calm everyone down, Lucinda tried assuring them that she was certain to turn up before the appointed time and she proceeded to prepare herself for the Earl's visit. But when her aunt, in some anxiety, came to tell her that the Earl had arrived and her father had requested their presence downstairs, Henrietta had still not been found.

Realising there was nothing to be done other than hope and pray she would turn up, in the meantime, in a state of apprehension, Lucinda made her way down to the drawing-room where her father was waiting with the Earl of Rainborough. When she entered her father came towards her, his face darkening with deep displeasure when he saw she was alone. He knew of Henrietta's absence from the house but did not believe she would be so discourteous as to deliberately go against his wishes and shun such an important guest as the Earl of Rainborough.

Laurence was standing in front of a large sofa with his back to Lucinda, studying with interest a portrait of her mother which hung above the fireplace. He felt Lucinda's presence in the room before he turned, having an odd, prickly feeling on the back of his neck. The sensation was so strong that he turned slowly and saw her.

Her stillness was like a positive force and there was something about her, something vital, and she held his attention across the room by the perfect picture she made, a lovely silhouette dressed in a modest gown of the deepest blue. He stared at her in astonished recognition, instantly remembering their previous, somewhat turbulent meetings, and he was unable to believe his good fortune—that this beautiful creature must be Sir Thomas's younger daughter.

Lucinda froze when she suddenly found herself staring into the Earl's face. With a shock that drew the breath from her lungs, she saw it was none other than the man she had met at the fair and, prior to that, in York—handsome, tall and lean, and unlike the other occasions when they'd met and his attire had been casual, today it was more formal. He was wearing a dark grey frock coat and knee breeches, his white silk waistcoat was delicately embroidered and a jabot spilled fine lace from his throat. Lucinda thought he looked more like a prince than an earl and he was even more handsome than she remembered. As she stared at him openly he regarded her with some amusement.

'May I present my daughter, Lucinda, Lord

Rainborough. Lucinda, this is the Earl of Rainborough.'

Quickly Laurence crossed over to her, bowing his head slightly but without taking his eyes from hers. There was a cool recklessness about his swarthy intelligent face and an imperceptible smile played on his lips—for he was clearly enjoying her obvious surprise and discomfiture at finding out he was the Earl of Rainborough after all. Sir Thomas, momentarily distracted by Celia entering the room, moved towards her to enquire about Henrietta, leaving the two of them alone.

'So—it is you again!' gasped Lucinda.

'It is. This is indeed a pleasant—and if I may say so—unexpected surprise,' he replied quietly, his voice deep.

'F-forgive me if I seem startled,' Lucinda stammered, 'but your presence here today has taken me wholly by surprise. Why—why did you not tell me who you were?'

'If I remember correctly, I did tell you. But— as I also remember—you did not believe me at the time. Is that not so?'

Lucinda flushed, remembering those awful things she had said to him, remembering, despite their contentious encounters, that as she had walked away from him that day, all she had wanted was to see him again and to talk to him. And now here he was, and the irony of it was that if her father had his way then he was about to become betrothed to her sister. She suddenly felt as if the whole world had been turned upside down.

'Tell me, are you always so disagreeable?' he asked with a wicked, secretive twinkle dancing in his dark eyes flecked with green.

'Some might say so.'

'Then I hope you are not going to be difficult today.'

'Usually I'm impossible,' she smiled, unable to resist the mischievous note in his voice. 'But not today. Today I promise to be on my best behaviour.'

'Then I am relieved to hear it,' he murmured.

'You know my daughter?' asked Sir Thomas, coming back to them.

'We met briefly at Rainborough fair but were not introduced,' explained Laurence. 'I feel I must compliment you, Sir Thomas. You have two charming daughters. Where is your other daughter—Henrietta? The young lady I met in London—the one we spoke of?'

'Lucinda—where is Henrietta?' her father asked. At the tight stricture of her face he nodded slightly, understanding fully that she had not as yet returned. But this he could not divulge to the Earl. 'Still getting ready, I don't doubt. The time these young ladies take over their toilet beggars belief,' he said to Laurence, laughing softly as he tried to make light of the situation, but the tension inside him was evident to Lucinda.

'My sister went riding earlier and was late back, my lord,' Lucinda explained, finding it odd and strangely irritating at having to address him as such, though it was correct, and hating having to make excuses for Henrietta, but there was nothing else for it that she could see. 'I daresay she will join us shortly.'

'Pray, do come and sit down, Lord Rainborough,' said Sir Thomas. 'Have refreshments brought in, will you, Celia?' he said to his cousin, hovering in the open doorway.

Although Sir Thomas's thick dark hair was now sparse and liberally streaked with grey and his once solid constitution, having lost its robustness, was now thin and hunched, in his black frock coat and polished black silver-buckled shoes and white silk stockings, he looked every inch the gentleman he was.

Lucinda took a seat opposite their guest. She was looking at him, fully alert, and her spine was straight, not even touching the back of her high-backed chair, graceful, registering everything that was said between her father and himself while her Aunt Celia presided over the tea things, an expensive beverage which her aunt had long since acquired a fondness for. Despite the ravages of the years and her ill health, which was a constant worry to them all, Celia was still tall and slim, looking regal in black silk. The Earl sat with one long lean black-booted leg crossed over the other, talking easily to Sir Thomas, but as he talked Lucinda was aware that he studied her absently.

The conversation was mostly about Rainborough and local matters, of anecdotes about acquaintances which were amusing and made both men laugh. They discussed politics—from the weary series of military campaigns still going on in Europe, bringing no visible prospect of peace, to Queen Anne's personal distaste for her ministers and estrangement from the Duchess of Marlborough. Their conversation somehow turned to Barbados and how things differed from life in England. At any other time Lucinda would have enjoyed imbibing such casual talk, especially on a subject so dear to her heart—she did so love hearing her father laugh and talk of his experiences as a plantation owner on Barbados—but today she was anxious, too nervous about what Henrietta was doing to concentrate on anything save how to prevent her tea from spilling into her lap and how to overcome the shock it had been on finding out who the Earl was.

The hands of the clock on the mantelpiece were creeping on and as time went by she felt her tension increase. Oh—where was

Henrietta? Why was she not here to welcome the Earl? Had she indeed run off with Hal Ingram? After all, she had implied that she might. She told herself not to be absurd, but once the random thought had entered her mind it gathered momentum and when she still did not appear she began to think there was some truth in the suspicion.

She glanced towards the door and then at her father, feeling a stirring of admiration for him; despite his displeasure over Henrietta's disobedience his dignity, as always, showed through.

Celia was momentarily called out of the room by one of the maids; when she returned her face was composed but as white as chalk.

'What is it, Celia?' enquired Sir Thomas.

Quickly she crossed to where he sat and handed him a note before going to stand by the window and looking out. Scanning the words on the piece of paper, Sir Thomas's face tightened and he clenched his hand that held the note, finding what he read both disturbing and intolerable.

'It seems my daughter will not be joining us after all. What can I say, Lord Rainborough, other than offer my deepest apologies? It appears she was taken ill whilst out riding and has retired to her room. She begs to be forgiven and sends her heartfelt apologies.'

Lucinda saw the Earl's lips tighten and a small frown made a furrow over the bridge of his nose, but then he smiled, cool and composed, knowing full well that for some reason her father was lying, that beneath the apparent calm of the room there was a tension that could be cut with a knife. But he was too much of a gentleman to mention it.

'Then what can I say other than I shall pray for her recovery. Please convey to her my good wishes.' He stood up suddenly. 'If you will forgive me I think it is time I left. I would have come to Burntwood Hall sooner but since coming to Rainborough there has been a multitude of things to do—and besides, I did not wish to impose myself on you uninvited.'

'You would have been more than welcome had you done so,' replied Sir Thomas.

Lucinda rose but did not accompany her father, who escorted the Earl to the door.

'I would like to repay your hospitality, Sir Thomas. You must visit me at Rainborough Castle and bring your daughter with you when she is recovered.' Laurence turned, expecting to find Lucinda beside her father, but when he saw she was still standing by her chair he retraced his steps across the carpet and stood looking down at her.

'Goodbye, Miss Howard. It has been a pleasure meeting you again.'

'Goodbye, my lord. I can only apologise for my rudeness on our previous meetings. Had I known who you were—'

'What?' he interrupted sharply. 'You would not have accused me of being unmannerly? Because I am an earl—which, I might add, I am still trying to come to terms with myself—does not mean you should not speak the truth.'

'Nevertheless, I should not have been so outspoken.'

'But you would have thought it all the same—and been correct in doing so. I believe in people speaking their minds, Miss Howard, and it may surprise you to know that I quite agree with you. My behaviour was unmannerly—and—like I said—I do promise to mend my ways. To make amends please allow me to invite you to Rainborough Castle along with your father and sister.'

'That is indeed kind of you, but there is no need for that,' Lucinda replied with a meaningful look. 'I am sure you would rather be alone with my sister.'

He frowned, studying her with those strongly arched eyebrows slightly raised. His gaze was penetrating and Lucinda was beginning to feel uncomfortable beneath it.

'So—you are still angry with me.'

'No. Of course not.'

'Then come. It will be a chance for us to get to know each other better.'

Lucinda met his eyes burning down into hers. 'But I don't think I want to get to know you better.'

'Why?' he said softly, for her ears alone, not in the least discouraged, for her reply did not surprise him in the least. 'Are you afraid you might get to like me?'

'Why should I be?' she replied, beginning to feel uneasy. 'Whether or not I like you is not an issue—and I am not afraid of anyone. Perhaps the soldiers under your command might be afraid of you but I certainly am not in that category.'

He smiled, a half-mocking, secretive smile. 'I do not mean it in that sense and I believe you know it. Goodbye, Miss Howard. I look forward to seeing you at Rainborough Castle.'

With a faint smile curving his lips, Laurence turned from her and crossed once more to where her father was waiting by the door. Lucinda watched them leave, deeply disturbed by his visit. She had not known many men in her life and the ones she had had been essentially gentle, but this man was different. He was arrogant and she had never liked arrogant men. He was a man of power and used to obedience from those about him.

Henrietta had been correct when she had

said he was excessively male and formidable. He was also sensual and, by the way he regarded her, Lucinda knew he was very much aware of her as a woman, which set her body tingling. She found him an attractive man and he was aware of this also. There was no doubt in her mind that she was disturbed by him. He made her feel uneasy and yet at the same time stimulated and excited.

If he were not a potential candidate for her sister's hand, then she would have said that he was set on a course of seduction where she was concerned, but she had no intention of falling victim to a philanderer. No wonder Henrietta, with her timid nature, was terrified of him. Her own common sense told her to think dispassionately about the Earl of Rainborough— especially if Henrietta was to marry him.

Lucinda's father returned to the room, his face grey and his eyes deeply troubled.

'What was the note, Father? What did it say?'

'It was from your sister. One of the servants found it on her dressing-table addressed to me. It seems she has done as she said and run off with Hal Ingram. She must be brought back before her escapade is the talk of Rainborough and her reputation in ruins.' He sighed, looking closely at Lucinda. 'Lord Rainborough seemed much taken with you, Lucinda. I did not realise you two had already met.'

'Well—as he said, our encounter was brief and not worth mentioning. We were not aware of each other's identity at the time.' She lowered her gaze, finding herself flushing beneath her father's searching gaze. Excusing herself quickly she left the room and only then did her father realise that he might have offered the wrong daughter in marriage to the Earl of Rainborough.

Laurence rode back to Rainborough Castle deep in thought. Whatever it was that had prevented Henrietta from meeting him that afternoon, he doubted very much that it had anything to do with ill health. When he had first met her in London he had admired her refinement of character, her charm and sensibility; in fact, there was nothing about her with which he could find fault, and he could not deny that he had been tempted by her father's proposition that she become his wife.

But since he had arrived at Rainborough, he had kept his eyes and ears open and there was not much that escaped his notice—especially not when Henrietta's name was being linked by the gossips to that of Hal Ingram from Carthwait. Not for one moment had he thought that she would reject him for some other—or that he would be untroubled by it.

After making the acquaintance of her sister,

he had come to desire Lucinda more. He had known that first moment he had set eyes on her in York that she was different from any other and, when she had walked into the room that afternoon, that his destiny was fixed.

Whatever Henrietta's reason for not being present that afternoon it did not bother him in the slightest, for to him Lucinda was pure perfection. He had experienced many liasons with the fair sex but none of any significance.

Lucinda had everything that was lacking in her sister—while Henrietta was timid and quiet, Lucinda was forthright and voluble. Not only did she possess beauty, a wonderful mane of fair hair and soft violet eyes in which a man could lose all reason, but also a quick brain. She said what she thought, and, he suspected, at times spoke the truth with an alarming disregard for whether the truth was acceptable to her audience or not.

To him she was lovely and fascinating. The unique qualities of her spirit and beauty appealed to him in a way no others ever had, promising a love beyond all his comprehension. As he rode away from Burntwood Hall, deep in thought for a man usually accustomed to the satisfaction of all his needs, he had already made up his mind to possess her.

# CHAPTER FOUR

HENRIETTA had indeed taken flight from
Burntwood Hall and the Earl of Rainborough,
and after his departure Lucinda soon became
aware of the circumstances. It seemed
Henrietta, regardless of the hurt and pain this
would cause her father, had gone to Hal
Ingram, pleading with him to take her away and
marry her before the formidable earl could be
foisted on her. Though it smote his heart to do
so, Hal had immediately returned her to her
father's fury, realising that to run off and get
married in the heat of the moment would harm
their cause and endear him even less to Sir
Thomas.

Angered by his daughter's behaviour, on her
return to Burntwood Hall Sir Thomas had
ordered her to her room directly and, loath as
he was to do so, had thanked Hal Ingram for
refusing to pander to his daughter's wishes. He
was grateful to him for refusing to marry her
without his consent, even though Henrietta was
of age. Reluctantly, Sir Thomas found himself
warming to this somewhat reserved young man,
who bore little resemblance to his brothers, and

he began to wonder if he might have misjudged him after all.

However, Sir Thomas was deeply worried and in a quandary as to what was to be done with his eldest daughter, who was presenting him with a wilful, stubborn side to her nature he hadn't known she possessed. Celia watched what was happening with a keen eye. Something must be done, that was for sure, and she sought to offer a solution to the unhappy affair, enlisting the aid of Lucinda, who was also sympathetic towards her sister's situation.

Tactfully, Celia broached the subject of Henrietta after dinner on the same day as the Earl's visit, when a tearful Henrietta was still in her room. Lucinda noticed how her father had sat hunched over his plate throughout the meal, with little interest for the food it held. He had said little since the Earl's departure as he sought a solution to what seemed to him to be a terrible dilemma, for nothing was turning out as he had planned.

'Forgive me, Thomas, if I speak out,' said Celia softly, unable to remain silent any longer on the subject. 'I'm sure you know what is best for your daughter—but the way I see it Henrietta should not be forced into a marriage she does not want. Oh, I know you have her best interests at heart—that the last thing you want is to see her unhappy.'

Sir Thomas raised his head and looked across the table at his cousin. 'What are you saying, Celia?'

'Let her have her way and marry Hal Ingram if that is what she wants,' she suggested gently. 'You know how fond she is of him—and he is a personable enough young man—not in the least like those incorrigible brothers of his—and his manners and behaviour cannot be faulted.' She sighed deeply. 'What's going to happen to this place when we're both gone, Thomas? Think of it. It saddens me when I think that strangers will come and live here. Why, there have been Howards living at Burntwood Hall for almost as long as Dwyers have been at Rainborough Castle.'

She sat back in her chair with a determined expression on her aged face, resolved that the decision she had made was the right one and would benefit them all.

'As you are aware, Thomas, when your father left England all those years ago for Barbados, his actions angered his father to such an extent that he cut off any claim he and his heirs might have to the estate. But now, seeing as the Howard estate belongs to me to dispose of as I think fit, then should you consent to Henrietta marrying Hal Ingram I shall bequeath it to them—making a settlement on Lucinda, also—although,' she said, looking across at Lucinda, 'you, my dear, I expect will make a prestigious marriage of your own.'

'Being the youngest of four sons, Hal will have little to come from his family, but from what I have seen of the Ingrams' land and the splendid way Hal has worked it—no doubt providing the money which enables his brothers and father to enjoy themselves so— then he has more than proved his worth. I feel sure that I would be leaving everything in good hands.'

Sir Thomas sat and listened to her, realising there may be some sense in what she was saying.

'If you're thinking of Lord Rainborough, Thomas, and the size of Henrietta's dowry she will take with her into marriage with any man, then I must tell you that Rainborough isn't the only estate that is suffering from neglect. Our own could do with some capital injecting into it. Come—what do you say?'

Lucinda rose from the table and went to her father, kneeling down beside his chair and taking his hand. Suddenly he looked very tired and so old. It had not escaped her notice that he had been coughing more than usual of late, and it sounded much worse. It tugged at her heart to see him like this. After a moment, a sad smile touched his lips and he sighed.

'Listen to Aunt Celia, Father,' she said gently. 'It does make sense.'

He sighed deeply, looking down into her upturned face. 'Dreams,' he murmured. 'Dreams. When your mother died I realised how wonderfully blessed I was to have two such beautiful daughters. I had such dreams, such high hopes for both of you. But that was not enough. What use are dreams without you have the time and will to carry them through? When I die, Lucinda, you and Henrietta will become extremely wealthy young ladies—a catch indeed for any fortune hunter. It is my intention to save you from that.

'My fortune has been acquired through ability and sheer hard work. I am determined not to let one penny piece go to a man whose first instinct will be to squander it on any form of gaming. I will only entrust you to men who will be worthy of you, who will take care of you and will be answerable for your future. Let it be understood that the reputation of the Ingrams' gives me cause to worry.'

'I know that, Father, but Hal is different from his brothers.'

'Yes—you may be right. Perhaps I have done the young man an injustice, judging him on the reputation of his family. He did bring Henrietta back today, refusing to do as she asked and marry her without my consent. He does have that to his credit.'

He looked at Lucinda with such sad, resigned eyes that it tore at her heart.

'I will talk to Henrietta. If she is set on marrying Hal Ingram then so be it—and—who knows—he might make her a good husband. It will also be a good thing to keep Burntwood Hall and the estate in the family.' He sighed deeply as he continued to look down at Lucinda. 'It may be too late to arrange a prestigious marriage for your sister but there is still you, Lucinda. I will give my mind over to that.'

Still kneeling beside his chair Lucinda stared at him and the decisive tone of his voice caused all the colour to drain out of her face. Before she had time to ask him what he meant he began coughing violently, which caused Celia to cross over to him in alarm. Slowly Lucinda rose to her feet, and only when his fit of coughing had subsided did she move away and leave them alone. As she climbed the stairs to her room, it was with a definite feeling of unease.

Lucinda's unease continued into the next day, for she felt the full weight of her father's words. What had he in mind? Was he to find a husband for her in the same way as he had tried for

Henrietta? She became fearful and apprehensive. Marriage was something she hadn't given much thought to, feeling she wouldn't have to consider this unpleasant situation until after Henrietta was married.

But her father's health was deteriorating by the day and she envisaged the man he chose not being agreeable to her—she had the sense to know that should this be the case, and if she objected as emotionally and stubbornly as Henrietta had done, then it could only hasten his demise. This she could not bear to think of. But one disturbing possibility occurred to her: supposing her father had a mind for her to marry the Earl of Rainborough instead of Henrietta? What would she do then? What could she do?

It was to escape these troubled thoughts that the following day she rode into Rainborough upon an errand for her aunt, riding side saddle on a spirited chestnut mare escorted by one of the grooms. She wore a pale green riding habit adorned with a deeper green braid and a fetching hat to match sat on her glossy curls.

Reluctant to return home after leaving Rainborough, and thinking her horse could do with a gallop, she set off in the direction of the woods. The sun was hot as she followed a forest path, riding under the luxuriant foliage of beeches and oaks, their dry leaves, some already carpeting the path, tinted with autumnal yellow and gold. Gaily she galloped off, leaving her groom cantering easily behind. Startled birds, disturbed by the pounding of her horse's hooves, took flight, fluttering and screeching into the sky.

She bent low over her horse's neck, revelling in the sudden coolness and the soft wind on her face, riding deeper into the forest, unaware that she had strayed further than usual until her surroundings ceased to be familiar. Suddenly the density of the trees brought a bitter chill to this twilight world.

From somewhere within the forest she heard the deep, throaty barking of dogs which she ignored until she heard them coming nearer. She began to feel uneasy, about to turn back when suddenly they burst out of the undergrowth like demons from hell, yapping and snarling, terrifying her poor mare so much that she bolted, carrying Lucinda, clinging on for dear life, deeper still into the forest, the dogs close on her horse's heels.

She was aware of someone following by the pounding of hooves behind her, of someone calling to the dogs. Suddenly her horse stumbled over a raised tree root and she was thrown from the saddle. Landing heavily, she was momentarily stunned by the impact of her fall onto the hard ground. When she opened her eyes her heart almost ceased to beat for she could only stare in horror as four huge ferocious hounds approached slowly, looking extremely dangerous. With their fangs bared they snarled, the biggest one edging forward, its hackles raised.

Holding her breath, Lucinda stared at them, paralyzed with fear. Terrified they would pounce and tear her limb from limb, knowing she must keep still, she prayed their master would come and call them off. As if in answer to her prayer suddenly a horse and rider came thundering through the trees, the man leaping from the saddle and hurrying towards her.

'Stay,' he roared at the dogs, but Lucinda barely heard the command over the wild pounding of her heart.

Immediately the dogs obeyed. They yelped and whimpered and sat back on their haunches, amazingly looking as harmless and innocent as a moment before they had looked like snarling monsters.

Lucinda closed her eyes and let her head fall back onto the ground, breathing a deep sigh of relief. The man approached and knelt beside her and when she opened her eyes it was to see the anxious face of the Earl of Rainborough bending over her.

'Are you all right?' he demanded.

'I—I don't know. The—the dogs—'

'Don't worry. They'll not harm you.'

'A moment ago I believed they would kill me. I might have known they would belong to you,' she said crossly. 'Do you not have any control over them?'

'To me they are faithful and obedient. The only people they usually encounter in these woods are trespassers—not often as charming as yourself, of course,' he said in a low voice and with a mischievous look in his dark eyes, 'and poachers.'

'Then the poachers have my heartfelt sympathy if they find themselves confronted by such monsters,' she retorted. 'Do you usually turn them loose like that?'

'Yes. You are forgetting that these are my woods. I am permitted to exercise my dogs as I see fit on my own land and, my dear Miss Howard,' he said with mock reproach, 'if you had not been trespassing, then you would not have been set upon.'

'Another minute and I dare say I would have been their dinner.'

'They just snarl and look intimidating to scare unwanted guests off my land.' He smiled faintly, his eyes narrowing. 'You do seem to have a genius for falling at my feet, Miss Howard. What am I to think?'

'Think what you like—only please make

those dogs stop looking at me as if I were their next meal.'

Laurence clapped his hands and the hounds retreated several yards away. From where she lay Lucinda saw that on account of the heat, above his tight, fawn-coloured breeches and knee-length boots, he was wearing only a fine white linen shirt, open at the neck, which revealed his strongly muscled throat. Feeling disturbed and somewhat embarrassed by this, suddenly she made a movement to get up, but his brown hand on her shoulder pressed her firmly back onto the ground.

'Wait—don't get up. Are you hurt anywhere?'

'No—I—I don't think so.'

She winced as she moved her head and Laurence noticed there was blood on her bonnet.

'Here—let me see,' he said, gently placing his fingers firmly on either side of her chin and turning her face to one side. Careful to keep any alarm out of his voice, he undid the satin ribbons and removed her bonnet.

'What is it? Is anything the matter?'

'It looks as if you've grazed the skin on the side of your face. Does it hurt?'

'No. It's a little sore—that's all.'

'Does your head ache?'

'I feel a little woozy—perhaps—but nothing more. Please help me to my feet.'

Placing his hands beneath her arms Laurence helped her to stand, but the effort caused her to sway against him. She felt dazed and dizzy with shock, with the ragged beating of her heart loud in her ears. Laurence held her with some concern as she breathed deeply, closing her eyes until it slowed to an even beat. She tried to pull away but his arms continued to hold her fast against him. His face was close to hers, making her all too aware of his nearness.

Her head reeled dizzily, mingling with other still more disturbing sensations, not altogether unpleasant, and she wondered if it were from the effects of the fall or suddenly finding herself in such close proximity to him, for she was conscious of the hardness of his muscles and of the masculine smell of his body—of leather and horses.

'I—I am so sorry,' she said faintly, continuing to abandon herself to his circling arms, for never had she been held in quite this way, with such resolute strength or with such a sense of security. 'I am ashamed to be so weak. I have taken many a tumble but this was especially hard. I shall be all right in a moment.'

'Take as long as you like,' he murmured with soft seduction, his lips against her hair, his arms tightening in a way that left no doubt as to the delight it gave him to hold her so close against him. 'For myself, I am quite content to go on holding you for as long as it is necessary.'

His words and the tone of his voice caused Lucinda instinctively to come to her senses and, breaking the spell, she disentangled herself from his arms and faced him. Drawn by the depths of her lovely violet eyes and the freshness of her soft lips, parted to reveal her moist, even teeth, noticing a little pulse beating madly beneath the whiteness of her skin in the rounded column of her throat, Laurence had to master a passion almost beyond his control not to draw her back into his arms.

Lucinda caught the passion in his dark eyes as they fastened on her lips, understanding all too well the innuendo behind his words. What she saw there was so obvious that she felt the colour rise in her cheeks. Because of her weakness, because her sudden attack of dizziness had caught her off her guard, she had been defenceless.

'I am sure you would,' she said coldly, trying to overcome her weakness, 'but I must be getting back. I have ridden further than I intended. I often ride into the woods—they are so beautiful—but I am not very familiar with this part.'

'Then you would have had difficulty finding your way back,' he reproached harshly. 'Surely you were not fool enough to ride into these woods alone? Don't you know that it is the height of dangerous folly? You could well have been set upon by cutthroats.'

'Not so fearsome to me as your pack of hounds,' she snapped. 'Of course I am not alone. A groom is with me but I rode on ahead.'

'Then it was reckless and irresponsible of him to let you out of sight.'

'Yes, I suppose it was,' she said, suddenly weary, turning to her horse, she moved towards it. Overcome by a fresh wave of dizziness, she placed her head against its soft neck, holding onto the bridle. Laurence went to her quickly, aware of her distress beneath the cool façade she had tried to present a moment before. She turned, noticing how extraordinarily tall and broad shouldered he suddenly seemed as he stood looking down at her, his eyes on her face, his expression grave and serious.

'Come—I will take you to Rainborough Castle. It isn't far and a good deal closer than Burntwood Hall. Mrs Foley, my housekeeper, will clean your wound. After you have rested, I will send you home in my carriage.'

'No—please—I would rather go home,' she said, her voice hesitant and at the same time tremulous.

'I will not hear of it. You will do as you're told and come with me,' he commanded. 'I cannot let you mount your own horse. See — she is restive and quivering. The fall, and, I have to say, her fear of the hounds, have unsettled her.'

Lucinda did not resist as he scooped her up into his arms and placed her on his magnificent black horse, hoisting himself up behind her just as a worried-looking groom emerged from the trees in search of Lucinda. Quickly Laurence told him what had occurred and that he was taking her to Rainborough Castle, instructing him to return to Burntwood Hall with her mount and explain what had happened, that Miss Howard was shaken but unhurt and he would return her safely after she had rested.

Followed by his hounds Laurence rode through the woods with his arms about Lucinda to support her.

'We'll soon be there,' he remarked, his lips close to her ear. 'As soon as we leave the woods we'll be in the castle grounds. Have you been there — to the castle?'

'No. I've never ventured further than the other side of the wood.'

'Then it will give me pleasure showing it to you — such as it is. You will see for yourself the neglect. There is much to be done but it will have to wait. First I must take care of the tenant farmers who depend on their farms for their livelihood. Their needs are greater than mine at this time.'

The trees were thinning out. As they rode into the glare of the sunlight, ahead of them, sitting on the summit of a gentle rise, was Rainborough Castle, the landscape being of undulating, uncultivated fields before giving way to purple moorland, the river curling about it on two sides like a lover's arm. It looked enormous and so grand and impressive, with flowering creepers and dark green ivy clinging in such profusion to its ancient walls that some of the leaded windows were almost obscured from sight.

Just as Lucinda had been told, the grounds and castle, with its surrounding wall tumbling down in places, were sorely in need of attention. But, strangely, in its neglected state she found a certain charm, an endearing quality in its lost look, and she felt privileged to have looked upon its beauty. But suddenly she felt reluctant to enter and could not say why. Half-alarmed, she wished she had not fallen in so readily with Lord Rainborough's suggestion that she go to Rainborough Castle, for she felt a general discomfort in going there.

Sensing what she was thinking, Laurence pulled the horse to a halt. 'Please—don't worry. I know how forbidding it must appear to you.'

'There I must contradict you. Why—it's

beautiful,' Lucinda breathed, almost forgetting his closeness. 'I've never seen anything like it.'

Laurence looked at her with a little smile, noting her parted lips and shining eyes, happy that it had made a favourable impression on her.

'I wish my cousin Rupert had thought so. Maybe if he had it would not be in such disrepair as it is now. Sadly, he preferred the smoke of London and the excitement of the gaming rooms to the peace and fresh air of Rainborough.'

As the horse resumed its walk, Lucinda hardly heard what he was saying as she watched the castle coming nearer. After crossing a hump-backed stone bridge over the gently flowing river, they rode beneath the shade of the trees and through the gates, finally stopping at the bottom of a wide stretch of stone steps leading up to two massive studded oak doors.

Laurence jumped down and, reaching up, lifted Lucinda to the ground. His warm strong grip disturbed her, making it more difficult to regard him as a mere acquaintance, and now that she was on his territory, at his home, she felt quite vulnerable. As she met his eyes she felt a sudden quickening inside her, which caused her to look away to where a man had just emerged from the house. It was William, the Earl's valet, who came down the steps to meet them.

'Ah, William, allow me to introduce to you Miss Howard.'

William greeted her politely with a smile of recognition. 'Ah, yes. I remember Miss Howard. We met at the fair.' He looked at Laurence sharply. 'Not Miss Henrietta Howard?'

'No. This is her sister—Miss Lucinda Howard, William. She's taken a tumble from her horse and is slightly hurt. I'll take her inside while you go in search of Mrs Foley. Ask her to come and attend to her, will you?'

Inside the ancient impressive hall Lucinda looked around in wonder, at the dark oak panelling, the walls hung with weapons and shields and, above the massive fireplace, the Dwyer coat of arms. As she stood there she felt all the past closing in on her, and that Laurence Dwyer was an important, essential part of it all—that without him all this would surely crumble.

'Welcome to Rainborough Castle, Miss Howard. It is without the pomp and grandeur which existed during my ancestors' time, and the hordes of servants employed to keep it going—but it's comfortable enough for the time being. Come into the drawing-room. I'm sure Mrs Foley won't be long.'

'Mrs Foley? She is your housekeeper?'

'She is, indeed. Mrs Foley is the mainstay of Rainborough Castle and has been the house-keeper for as long as anyone can remember—as her mother was before that. She rules like a matriarch and commands the respect of servants and family alike. As unruly, troublesome boys, both Rupert and I were oft chastised by her, for like the servants we were not spared any infringement.'

Inside the drawing-room, Lucinda gazed around at the gilt-framed pictures and mirrors adorning the walls, at the polished, ornately carved furniture which had been in the Dwyer family for generations, at velvet draperies, at sofas and chairs, some beautifully upholstered, some faded and worn with time but which could easily be renovated.

A small plump woman entered the room, carrying a tray on which were a bowl of water, lint and a pot of salve with which to cleanse Lucinda's wound. She had bright grey-blue eyes and iron grey hair, drawn into a tight bun beneath a white laced cap. Her kindly face was wreathed in smiles at the sight of Laurence. It had been a sad day when the old Earl had died, followed so closely by master Rupert. But it had been a happy one when master Laurence—always her favourite—had come to take over, and she suspected that Rainborough was in for better times. The hopes and continuation of the Dwyers depended on him, and if anyone could make a success of such an unenviable undertaking then he could.

'Miss Howard is from Barbados, Mrs Foley,' explained Laurence when they had been introduced and she had settled herself beside Lucinda, beginning to tend her wound.

'Aye, that I know. There's little one doesn't know in Rainborough, especially when newcomers arrive. How is your father, Miss Howard? I hear he hasn't been too well these past months.'

'No. He—he doesn't enjoy the best of health, I'm sorry to say. Although today is one of his better days.'

'Then it's glad I am to hear it. And Lady Celia? How is she these days?'

'Sadly, she also suffers from ill health—but she is not a complainer and when you ask how she is feeling she always replies that she is better today. However—there are times when I know this is not so. Lord Rainborough tells me that you have lived at the castle for a long time, Mrs Foley?'

'Oh, aye, that I have. I was born here and no doubt I shall die here. There's been members of my family at the castle in one way or another almost as long as the Dwyers. Is that not so, Master Laurence?'

Laurence laughed good humouredly. That Mrs Foley continued to address him as she had when he'd been a boy he found amusing and rather touching. 'It certainly is, Mrs Foley.'

Lucinda saw that Mrs Foley enjoyed treating Lord Rainborough as she had when he'd been a boy. Observing him in this relaxed atmosphere, she noticed that when he threw back his head and laughed at what Mrs Foley had said his face seemed much younger, less harsh and sardonic, as it did when in repose.

'I remember your grandfather, Miss Howard. A fine, handsome man he was—and proud, too. Oh—there was many a time he would come here—with always a kind word for everyone. I remember how he took off for Barbados with his family all those years ago—and who could blame him? Better that, he said, than be ground down beneath the heel of Cromwell's boot. I was only a girl at the time but I remember it well. That I do. Now—how did you come to fall off your horse like that?'

Lucinda cast a reproachful glance in Laurence's direction. He was standing leaning lazily against an immense fireplace, one booted foot resting on the hearthstone, watching as Mrs Foley gently cleansed the wound on her face. A thick lock of hair fell rebelliously over his forehead. His gaze shifted to her eyes and, seeing her look of gentle reproach, he arched his eyebrows with amusement and a smile curved his mouth.

'I think his lordship is best qualified to answer that.'

'I'm afraid that was all my fault,' he admitted. 'The hounds startled Miss Howard's horse, which caused it to bolt. Unfortunately, Miss Howard's horsemanship must be somewhat lacking otherwise she would not have fallen off. Do they not teach young ladies to ride properly on Barbados, Miss Howard?'

Lucinda's eyes opened wide in amazement at his rudeness. 'Oh!' she exclaimed, 'I resent that,' but when she saw his crooked smile and how his deep green-brown eyes danced then she realised he was jesting. She sighed and her lips broke into a smile.

'Why, there is no fault with my horsemanship, my lord—and the ladies on Barbados ride as well as any English miss. And, anyhow, as I remember it my horse stumbled. His lordship has a habit of making accidents happen, Mrs Foley. It is not my first encounter with his reckless ways—is it my lord? Why—the first time we met in York he quite literally swept me off my feet—which resulted in a sprained ankle that time. I was not even mounted on a horse, either.'

Laurence raised his eyebrows. 'Why do you smile? I assure you it was not deliberate.'

'Deliberate or not—you did knock me over,' she chastised.

Mrs Foley listened to their light banter with keen interest and amusement, and if she did not already know that Master Laurence was to make a proposal of marriage to Miss Henrietta Howard, this young lady's sister, then she would have thought she was listening to a light-hearted tiff between two lovers.

'Pay no attention to his lordship. That's just like him,' she said. 'He's acquired many peculiarities whilst battling with so many men of different nationalities from all around the globe that he is lamentably ignorant of the etiquette which should prevail while in the company of a lady. He's used to commanding a regiment— ordering what has to be done and expecting his commands to be obeyed in an instant.'

'Army life instils that kind of discipline into a man, Mrs Foley. I cannot change the habits of a lifetime.'

'Habits or your manners, my lord?' retorted Lucinda.

'You tell me, Miss Howard?' he asked, his voice low, his eyes fastened on hers. 'Is there hope, do you think, for a transformation from an ill-mannered soldier to a gentleman? Can I be anything else?'

'If a child can change its manners, then I dare say there should be hope for you.' Lucinda

avoided the direct questioning of his eyes and
gave Mrs Foley a brilliant smile, who had just
finished cleansing the graze on her face. 'Thank
you, Mrs Foley. You have been very kind. I'm
sure there won't be a sign of it in a few days.'

'Aye—well—I hope you're right. You've
such a pretty face. Now—you rest there awhile
and get over your fall. I'll just go to the kitchen
and get you some refreshment. I'm sure you
could do with it.'

'That would be very nice. I'm feeling much
better already.'

# CHAPTER FIVE

WITH Mrs Foley's disappearance to the domestic quarters Laurence's mood changed. He fell silent, his expression grave.

'As you are feeling better,' he said at length, moving towards her and speaking somewhat harshly, 'come out onto the terrace. There is a matter I wish to speak with you about.'

Before Lucinda could reply he had taken her out onto the terrace where a short flight of steps led down to the gardens below. A profusion of delicate pink roses tumbling over a trellis caught her eye and she looked at them dreamily, moving towards them, better to smell their intoxicating scent.

'What are you thinking?' Laurence asked after a moment, breaking in on her reverie, seeing the softness on her face and a certain sadness enter her eyes.

She sighed. 'I was thinking of my home on Barbados. We had roses just like these.'

'So—you are homesick,' he remarked, correctly guessing the cause of her sadness.

'Yes. It seems so very far away now. I was born there—I lived there all my life and I shall

95

always regard it as my home. I had no wish to leave — ever.'

The memory of her departure from Barbados still hurt dreadfully, for she remembered how, with each mile taking her further away, she had experienced a strong sense of loss and isolation because she was leaving her childhood and all the happiness she had ever known behind. She had been swamped with an unhappiness so acute that it had been like a bereavement, failing to understand her father's reasons when he had told her and Henrietta that he had decided to sell everything and move to England.

But now she knew that, after the death of their mother, whom he had adored, with his increasing ill health and his yearning to be back in the land of his ancestors, nothing would have persuaded him to stay. She could not tell Lord Rainborough that it had almost broken her heart to leave Barbados, far more deeply than any man ever could.

But she did not have to tell him; what she felt was there in her eyes for him to see, and in a strange way he felt an odd sense of identity with her, as if they were two of a kind, trying to hold on to something that was infinitely precious.

He nodded slowly, seeing her eyes suddenly swim with tears. 'Let me show you the gardens,' he sad brusquely. 'They are sadly in need of straightening up but they are pleasant to walk through, just the same.'

Grateful to him for giving her a moment to rid herself of her melancholy and compose herself, Lucinda followed him down the steps. Despite the neglected state of the gardens, the wild tangle of weeds and rampant brambles covering the walls, she could see how it must have looked at one time, and, if Lord Rainborough had his way, would one day look again.

They walked down a path past a flagged stone circle with a sundial, framed by bay trees which had once been clipped short, moving through a rose-covered gateway into a walled garden where in times past rows of vegetables would have awaited the cook's delicate touch in the kitchen. Low hedges lined the pathways to a henhouse by the orchard where chickens wandered at will, and close by were beehives, ensuring an extra crop of apples and pears because of the pollination by the bees.

'This old kitchen garden has supplied the castle with fresh fruit and vegetables for centuries. As you can see, it will be some time before it can be restored—as will everything else,' Laurence explained with a note of regret. 'Much as I loved my cousin Rupert, most of it has to be put down to his own mismanagement.

He proved to be incompetent and extravagant to excess.'

'I see you have much to do.'

He gave her a wry smile. 'A new task is always a challenge.'

Lucinda paused and looked up at him. 'You said you wanted to speak to me. What about?'

Her question caused his face to harden, bearing no resemblance to the man who had welcomed her to his home just a short while before. She wondered what it could be that had brought about this change. His dark eyes glittered coldly and seemed to look deep into her heart.

'Yes, I did. It is the matter concerning your sister. There is something I would like you to explain—why she chose not to see me when I called on her at Burntwood Hall yesterday?'

'Oh!' gasped Lucinda, somewhat put out, for this was a matter she would prefer not to discuss. 'But she did. She—she was indisposed, that is all.'

Laurence's eyes narrowed and his lips curled with scorn. 'Miss Howard—do not take me for a fool. What does this mean? Come—something has changed since I last saw her in London. I have to say that I have heard the gossip concerning her and Hal Ingram. Has this anything to do with her behaviour towards me?'

His eyes were on Lucinda, watching her face

closely. She was unnerved by it and lowered her gaze to cover her confusion.

'Do—do you know the Ingrams?' she asked hesitantly.

'Yes. They always were a wild bunch. I know Hal is a penniless fourth son who, unlike his father and brothers, who have taken to gaming and laying bets on anything in the hope of improving their affairs, is more interested in running the farm. Does your sister have any romantic notions for Hal?'

Beneath his direct gaze and close questioning Lucinda became flustered. 'This really is a delicate matter, my lord, one I do not think you should be discussing with me. It is my father you should be speaking to. But, as you ask, then yes, Henrietta is quite enamoured of him. Unfortunately, before Father took her to London to speak with your lawyer, she failed to convey to him the depth of her love for Hal— the completeness of it.'

'I see. Your father does not approve of him, I take it? Otherwise he would not have approached my lawyers.'

'My father has always been a careful man where money is concerned and the reputation of the Ingram family is such that he has need to worry.'

'And Hal Ingram is different?'

'Yes. He is considerate and kind and loves

Henrietta dearly. Father will have to revise his opinion of him and allow them to marry otherwise Henrietta will never be truly content. She has gone through life with a serene acceptance of all things. That she is fighting now with tooth and nail reveals the depth and strength of her feelings. Father will have to let her have her way.'

Laurence nodded grimly. 'I see. It is clear to me that your father made the proposal that I consider marriage to your sister without a thought to her finer feelings. However— nothing was signed and no promises made. But I cannot deny that this changes matters considerably. Should your father broach the matter again regarding marriage to Henrietta, then I would be forced to refuse. I would not even contemplate marrying a woman whose heart was elsewhere.'

'What? Not even to save your precious Rainborough?'

'No. Not even to save Rainborough,' he said with icy calm. 'I am not the mercenary you obviously take me for, Miss Howard. Forgive me if I am blunt but, without the dowry which your sister would have brought with marriage, I will have to sell some land and build the estate up gradually over the years. But one thing I will not do—sell Rainborough outright. And yes, it is precious to me—as precious to me as Barbados so clearly is to you.'

'It is unfortunate for you that Henrietta's heart lies elsewhere—I can see that—for I do realise that marriage to her would have been a solution to your problems. But I have to say that, if Father does not treat her too harshly and allows her to marry Hal Ingram, I shall be happy for her, for, as seems to be common among the English aristocracy, I frown upon marriages arranged without reference to the feelings of the bride—with sole regard to the increase of family fortunes.'

Laurence's face might have been carved out of stone when he fastened his hard gaze on hers and there was a saturnine twist to his mouth. 'And what of yourself, Miss Howard? Is this not what your father intends for you? An arranged marriage? Finding yourself in your sister's situation, how will you react if you do not approve of his choice? Will you also go against his wishes and fight tooth and nail?'

Lucinda looked at him directly. 'I have never defied my father, Lord Rainborough. I love him dearly and understand perfectly why it is so important to him that Henrietta and I make suitable marriages. Unlike my sister, I am not in love with another—so—when the time comes it will not be as difficult for me to accept. But surely it is not all that bleak for you?'

Laurence frowned, his eyes narrowing. 'What do you mean?'

'Why—there is nothing to stop you looking for another heiress to marry. A generous dowry in exchange for the grand title of Countess of Rainborough. There must be hundreds with ambitious parents who would be only too ready to offer their daughters for an increase in position.'

'I do not doubt that for one moment,' Laurence said dryly.

'In the light of Henrietta's reluctance to marry you, it might prove beneficial for you to return to London where there will be any number of suitable young ladies to choose from.'

'Having only recently arrived from there, I have no desire to return so soon. I have far too much to do here at present. Besides,' he said, sighing deeply as his eyes passed over the wild tangle of the gardens, 'before I bring any pro-spective bride to Rainborough I ought to set about bringing some semblance of order to the place. So much neglect and disorder is enough to send any well brought-up young lady running back to her mother in despair.'

His words caused Lucinda to smile, a softness entering her eyes as she too looked about her. 'I don't think you need worry. The stables may not be filled with horses and the house may be in need of repair, the gardens something of a wilderness—the encroachment of nature all too evident—but beauty and charm has been born out of its neglect. Mellowed by the years, it wears a look of welcome and warmth no one could fail to be aware of. I'm sure whoever you choose to marry will fall in love with Rainborough.'

Laurence's green-brown eyes rested on her face with genuine warmth. 'Do you really mean that?'

Lucinda met his gaze without embarrassment. 'Of course. I would not have said it if I did not mean it.'

'Then perhaps I won't have to return to London after all, Miss Howard,' he murmured, with a strange look in his eyes that Lucinda could not comprehend just then. 'I may have exactly what I'm looking for right here in Rainborough after all.'

He was smiling now as Lucinda looked at him but before she could ask him what he meant by that he took her arm, looking towards the house.

Their conversation was interrupted by Mrs Foley gesturing to them from the terrace, indicating that she had prepared refreshment, but later, travelling in Lord Rainborough's carriage back to Burntwood Hall, Lucinda reflected on it and was deeply troubled. The banter of words

that went on between them as Mrs Foley had
tended her wound had been a kind of mental
seduction she had never experienced with any
other man before, but since the moment she
had told him he would have to look for another
heiress to marry he had been quiet and
preoccupied.

Often she had found him studying her
closely—as her father had done when he
realised that Henrietta could no longer be considered as a prospective bride for the Earl of
Rainborough. But it was absurd to think he
would even consider marrying her. The Earl of
Rainborough—handsome, distinguished, hero
of many battles abroad, who could have the
pick of any beautiful heiress he desired—why
would he even contemplate choosing her?

But what if he did suggest marriage to her?
What would she do? she asked herself in some
consternation. Her common sense told her that
she would have to think very dispassionately
about it before she entered into such a relationship, but there were so many conflicting themes
in her heart and mind that she was confused.
Why had she let her emotions become
involved? The truth of it was that she had and
she greatly feared that she would become overwhelmed by him.

Not for the first time a mental picture of the
young foreign woman he had been with in York

came to mind and she thought it strange that he had not mentioned her. Who was she? She could not be his wife, otherwise he would not have considered marriage to Henrietta. He had just returned from Spain, she was clearly of that country, and they had seemed extremely familiar with each other. Was it possible that she might be his mistress?

Lucinda thrust this thought from her mind, afraid to analyse the strong rush of resentment she felt towards the young woman just then. But of one thing she was quite sure. He attracted her more than any man before but also he emanated a power, a commanding personality, no doubt due to his military training, which drew her to him. He was also proud, sardonic and harsh, which were traits which would have repulsed her in anyone else—but all this was an irresistible element of the attraction she felt for the Earl of Rainborough.

Lucinda arrived back at Burntwood Hall in a thoughtful mood. After reassuring her father and aunt Celia that she was quite all right after her fall, that she had sustained nothing more serious than a slight graze to her face, she went to her room where Henrietta sought her out.

'Here you are!' she exclaimed, with her eyes sparkling and her pallor of the past weeks replaced by a glow which tinted her fully rounded cheeks, because her father had at last relented and allowed Hal Ingram to call on her. Clearly Lucinda's time spent at Rainborough Castle had piqued her curiosity, for she was eager to know all that had transpired between her and the Earl of Rainborough. Throwing herself onto the bed, she looked up at her sister excitedly.

'So—you have been to Rainborough Castle, Lucinda, with the fearsome Lord Rainborough. What's it like? Is it as dilapidated as everyone says?'

Lucinda shrugged slightly, irritated by the eager, inquiring expression on her sister's face for she was in no mood for a barrage of questions.

'It's certainly in need of some repair—but it's a lovely old place all the same.'

'Did Lord Rainborough show you around?'

'No, not really. The time I was there was taken up by his housekeeper tending the graze on my face—although—he has promised to show me the castle on another occasion.'

Henrietta sat up and looked at her younger sister more keenly now. 'Oh—so you are to return? I—I suppose it's safe to presume you're not compromised by your visit there today?'

Lucinda stared at her, her face becoming suffused with a wave of crimson and her thoughtful manner giving way to a most earnest indignation.

'Of course not. What on earth prompted you to ask that?'

Observing Lucinda's change of colour, Henrietta smiled mischievously. 'Well—you were gone for so long and you have to admit that he is most eligible, Lucinda—but for his lost inheritance, of course.'

'And the fact that he can be both arrogant and conceited—and has too high an opinion of himself,' Lucinda replied heatedly in her attempt to conceal the confusion she was feeling since returning to Burntwood Hall.

'Come now, you are a terrible liar, Lucinda. Anyone can see you're attracted by him—and I am sure you are more to his taste than I. As for myself and the very idea that Father intended that I should marry him—well—let's just say that I put that down to an unpleasant experience.'

'Henrietta! How can you say that?'

'Why on earth not? It's true, isn't it? Oh, he is charming, though, and incredibly hand-some—despite his polite reserve and the fact that he terrifies me half to death.'

'You may be terrified of him, Henrietta, but I certainly am not.'

'Oh? Then what are your feelings with regard to him?' persisted Henrietta.

Relenting, Lucinda sighed deeply, sitting beside her sister on the bed and confiding some of the thoughts that were beginning to trouble her so.

'I don't know, Henrietta. Truly—I have no idea how I feel. But what I do know is that there is something between us that seems to draw us together. He fills me with such confusion that I do not know what to think. He has a habit of encroaching on my thoughts when I least expect it and, no matter how hard I persist in driving him out, he returns. Alas, Lord Rainborough is all you said he was, and much more, and it seems I am not nearly as immune to his masculinity as I thought I was—or as I wanted to be.'

There was a note of such unhappiness in Lucinda's voice that Henrietta leaned over and kissed her cheek affectionately. 'Then do not worry about it, Lucinda. Come—if it distresses you to discuss this then we will talk of other matters—but are you sure you're not just a little bit in love with him?' she asked hesitantly.

'Henrietta!' Lucinda exclaimed sharply. 'How could I be?'

'Well—it would be convenient if you were, wouldn't it? At least then Father would be satisfied.'

'No, Henrietta, it would not be convenient. I will not marry Lord Rainborough. I have no

intention of becoming involved with any man
who will see me as little more than a means of
paying his debts and financially securing his
future. There has to be more to marriage than
that.'

'But you said yourself that when you are
together there are vibrations between the two
of you, so it is plain that he is attracted by you.
Has he given you any indication to suppose that
he might want to get to know you better?'

'Lord Rainborough has made no advances
towards me whatsoever, Henrietta. And now I
would be obliged if you would refrain from
discussing this matter further. It has been a long
day and my head is beginning to ache.'

Judging it advisable to do as Lucinda asked,
Henrietta continued to prattle on about the
subject closest to her heart—Hal Ingram. But
as Lucinda continued to think of Lord
Rainborough during the days following her visit
to Rainborough Castle her manner became
quiet and subdued and she seemed edgy and
out of sorts, which brought Celia's observant
eyes upon her. Celia regarded her with careful
scrutiny, for she sensed that Lord Rainborough
was somehow responsible for this odd
behaviour.

As the long summer days slowly slipped almost
unnoticed into autumn, an invitation arrived

from Lord and Lady Lampton, close friends of
Celia's, inviting her to spend a few days with
them. Their home, Easterlea Manor, was situated twenty miles away on the coast which,
because of the poor quality of the roads, was a
good half-day's journey or more from
Rainborough. The invitation was extended to
include both Henrietta and Lucinda, expressing
a desire that they would be delighted to meet
them both.

Celia was frequently invited to join small,
diverting weekend parties at neighbouring
houses, but recently age and ill health often
kept her away. However, this was one invitation
she was determined to accept, for she had a
strong instinct that the visit could prove beneficial to Lucinda.

'I have received an invitation from Lord and
Lady Lampton,' she told both girls when they
were together. 'They are old friends of mine
and have recently returned to Yorkshire from
London. They have expressed a desire that I go
and stay with them for a short while—and
they would be delighted for you both to accompany me. Come—what do you say? Does the
prospect of going to Easterlea not appeal to
you?'

Celia could tell by the expression in
Lucinda's eyes that she was not averse to the
idea of spending a few days away from

Rainborough, but Henrietta's countenance fell at the very idea of being so far away from her precious Hal—if only for a few days.

'That's very kind of Lord and Lady Lampton, Aunt Celia,' said Lucinda. 'I hear Easterlea is quite magnificent and would love to see it.'

'Good, then that is settled. I will send word that we will be pleased to accept their invitation.'

Henrietta, who had remained unduly quiet, spoke out at last. 'Would you mind if I didn't go? I do not feel in the least like visiting at this time—and nor do I like the idea of Father being left alone. You go, Aunt Celia, you and Lucinda.'

Celia nodded, accepting her refusal to go without argument. 'As you wish, Henrietta. I do understand your apprehension and concern for your father and you are right. It would be unwise to leave him here alone. Lucinda and I will go—just for two or three days—no more. We do tend to live in comparative isolation here in the country,' she said to Lucinda, 'compared to city folk. You have been looking rather pale of late, my dear, and been far too quiet. It will do you good to be by the sea for a while and to meet other people before winter sets in.'

Her aunt was right, Lucinda thought, for there had been little in the way of entertainment since they had come to England—except for the short time spent in London when they had first arrived, the occasional visit to York and the odd diverting house party at one of her aunt's acquaintances. Last winter, as was usual most winters in England, they had seldom gone abroad at all, except in the neighbourhood of Rainborough, for travelling was both dangerous and difficult, the roads being deep in mud and often impassable. Visiting friends for any kind of jollification was viewed with apprehension, for it could mean spending the night with them or several nights if the weather turned bad.

'What are Lord and Lady Lampton like?' asked Lucinda, curious and surprised by her aunt's eagerness to accept this invitation, since she had been reluctant to undertake any form of travel of late because of her ill health. She could only assume that Celia was feeling a good deal better and in need of a little recreation.

'Oh, you'll like them, I know. Lord Lampton's hospitality is open handed and he has an ardent love of horses and hounds, with a gargantuan appetite for beef and ale, while Lady Lampton, a good many years younger than he, enjoys nothing better than indulging her passion for entertaining—which she does superbly and on a truly grand scale. No doubt there will be several guests from London staying at Easterlea so we must go through your wardrobe to make quite certain you will be suitably attired. It is imperative that you look your best. After all,' she said with a definite twinkle in her eye, 'there is no knowing who one is likely to meet.'

Contrary to what her aunt had in mind, Lucinda was not going to Easterlea to meet anyone. She merely wanted to be consigned to oblivion for just a few days, to move away from Rainborough—away from the disturbing presence of Lord Rainborough, for she found herself thinking of him, thinking and dwelling on snatches of their conversation and flushing softly when she saw again in her mind's eye the quiet, strange expression in his eyes when she had bade him farewell at Rainborough Castle, and remembered the firm, warm clasp of his fingers gripping hers as he had assisted her up into the carriage which was to take her back to Burntwood Hall. Silently she reproached herself for foolishly thinking of him all the time and forced herself to concentrate on her visit to Easterlea.

# CHAPTER SIX

SEATED across from her aunt Celia, Lucinda felt a curious thrill of excitement as the carriage left the small town of Easterlea behind. The long golden day spilled into evening, and the familiar salt sea smell drenched the air like a balm to her whole being, starved as she was of her island home where the sea had played such an integral part of her life.

Easterlea Manor, ancestral home of Lord Lampton, lay beyond the town, cupped in a little valley on the east coast. Lucinda watched the house draw closer. Built of local stone in Tudor times, which had mellowed to a rich gold, the immense, sprawling house, topped by turrets and innumerable chimneys, was surrounded by a ring of trees which gave way to gardens and terraces with clipped evergreens and leaden statues. Over the rise of the hill stretched the shimmering waters of the North Sea.

They were met by Lady Lampton in the wide welcoming hall which was decked with flowers and pleasantly cool. At thirty-five, Beatrice Lampton was tall and regal and immaculately

114

HELEN DICKSON 115

groomed, her hair as dark as were her eyes.
There was a firmness about her features and to
the set of her jaw that revealed her strength of
character. It was a similarity Lucinda had seen
in someone else—that someone else being Lord
Rainborough.

Having determined to put a distance between
Lord Rainborough and herself, to banish him
from her mind whilst spending a tranquil few
days at Easterlea, Lucinda was amazed at the
intensity of feeling this similarity evoked, and
she rebuked herself severely for allowing her
mind to weaken so easily and think of him.

It was clear to Lucinda that there was a
fondness between her aunt and Lady Lampton
as she watched them embrace warmly.

'My dear Celia,' said Lady Lampton. 'How
good it is to see you again and how glad I am
that you felt well enough to make the journey.
You are feeling better, I hope?'

'Yes, thank you, Beatrice. Some days are
better than others—but,' she said with a note of
wistful regret, 'I am not getting any younger so
I suppose it is only to be expected.'

Lady Lampton's eyes moved past Celia to
where Lucinda stood and her lips broke into a
welcoming smile.

'And you, my dear, must be Lucinda.'
Moving towards her she looked down at her
with a great deal of interest, studying her fea-

tures closely. 'It gives me great pleasure to welcome you to Easterlea and to say how delighted I am to meet you at last—having heard all about you—and I must say that you are every bit as beautiful as I was told you would be. I am sorry Henrietta was unable to accompany you.'

'It was kind of you to invite us, Lady Lampton,' Lucinda replied, thinking how cool and poised their hostess was, 'but Henrietta was reluctant to leave Father alone. He has not been at all well of late.'

'Then I am sorry to hear it.'

'Unfortunately, because of Sir Thomas's ill health, Beatrice, we are unable to stay more than two or three days at the most,' Celia told her.

'Then we must see to it that your visit is made as enjoyable as possible—otherwise the journey will hardly seem worthwhile.'

'Are we the first of your guests to arrive?' asked Celia.

'No—the last—apart from my cousin, that is. No doubt he will arrive some time tomorrow. Along with other guests, Lord and Lady Skelton arrived from Berwick yesterday, as did Sir Stephen Berrisford and his wife Emily with their daughter Amelia. You remember Sir Stephen, don't you, Celia? From Newcastle?'

'Of course—although it is many years since I last saw them.'

'They are to spend a few days here with us at Easterlea before travelling on to London for the winter months. How I envy them,' she said, sighing wistfully, smiling softly when she saw Lucinda's puzzlement at her remark. 'Life can be intolerably dull in the country during the winter months, Lucinda,' she explained. 'Most of the gentry migrate to London at this time—but Cedric, my dear husband, will not hear of it.'

'How is Cedric?' enquired Celia.

'Better now he's back in his beloved Yorkshire. How he detests the constant round of masques and balls he has to endure when we're in London. As yet I am still unable to pry him away from Easterlea during the winter months when hunting is at its best—and so I must endure the drearyness of country life as best I can.' The good-natured tolerance with which she endured her adored husband's love of Easterlea caused her to smile softly.

'Cedric is never happy unless he's at the reins, hurtling over fences in pursuit of stag or fox—it matters not one iota which—in the wake of a pack of hounds. How he doesn't take a tumble and break his neck I'll never know. He says he sends his heart over first and follows as best he can, so with that I have to be content.

'You'll meet him later, Lucinda. At this time he is to be found either at the stables with his hunters—which, I might add, he cossets as one would a child, or the kennels with his hounds—of which he is immensely proud—declaring there isn't another pack like it in the whole of Yorkshire. Come,' she said, moving towards the staircase, 'enough of Cedric. I will show you to your rooms. I'm sure you would like to refresh yourselves after your journey and to rest before dinner.'

As Lucinda followed Lady Lampton and her aunt up a curving staircase to a gallery above the hall she thought back to Lady Lampton's greeting with some puzzlement. She had mentioned that she had heard all about her, which was curious, for she could only know what her aunt had told her and, as far as she was aware, they did not correspond all that regularly, although her aunt often spoke of her. But if it was not her aunt who had told Lady Lampton about her, then who could it be?

She was puzzled and suspicious, suspecting that something was afoot, but in her excitement at being at Easterlea she put it out of her mind.

When Lucinda and her aunt emerged from their rooms and went downstairs, refreshed after resting from their journey, it was to find a full complement of guests already assembled. The party was a definite social event for Lady Lampton, who, unable to winter in London, had to console herself with these gatherings at Easterlea.

Lucinda was presented to Lord and Lady Skelton, both stout and middle-aged, who shared a love of country pursuits which endeared them to Lord Lampton, a squat, earthy-looking gentleman with a ruddy complexion and such an easy, friendly manner, if somewhat bellicose, that it was impossible not to like him.

And then there was the extremely wealthy Sir Stephen and Lady Emily Berrisford, and their daughter Amelia—a perfect picture of sweetness, nymph-like and demure, with soft, pouting lips and languishing periwinkle blue eyes and a peach-like complexion. Her thick golden ringlets framed her angelic heart-shaped face and bobbed about enchantingly when she moved and tossed her head—which she did frequently for it achieved the desired effect of attracting everyone's admiring attention—a movement which most men found irresistible.

Lucinda considered her to be a vain, silly, frivolous creature, often given to uncontrollable fits of girlish giggles, and when she became excited her voice rose to a high pitch which Lucinda found extremely irritating. She was watched over by her indomitable mother, a thin, sharp-featured woman who realised the importance of getting her only daughter introduced into society. And where better than London, where she would be launched onto the marriage market to display her assets. She was full of determination not to let her only daughter languish away in the stultifying countryside when all the eligible young men could be found in London, for she had high hopes that Amelia would marry into the aristocracy.

Apart from Miss Amelia Berrisford, Easterlea suited Lucinda very well and she made up her mind to avoid the young lady whenever possible—which proved to be easier said than done. The following morning, when she was preparing to go into Easterlea with Nancy to do some shopping and view the castle, to her dismay Amelia was of the same mind, so the three of them went off together. Celia preferred to remain in her room and rest to recover from the rigours of the previous day's journey.

The town of Easterlea was dominated by its Norman castle, and its muddle of cottages intertwined and clustered around the busy market place from which cobbled wynds threaded from street to street. It was a beautiful morning, the weather pleasantly warm. After leaving the carriage and driver just on the outskirts of

Easterlea, Lucinda was content to stroll and browse but she was never free of Amelia's animated chatter about the wonderful time she was going to have in London and the important families she would meet and associate with, and the armies of young gentlemen who would be seeking her hand in marriage. Lucinda found it all so tiresome and was beginning to regret her decision to visit the town, but somehow she managed to maintain her calm and listened politely, answering in monosyllables which seemed sufficient to make Amelia happy.

In the shadow of the crumbling castle they wandered through the narrow cobbled streets looking in the shop windows, stopping occasionally to go inside and purchase a trinket or two. When they threaded their way among the busy market stalls clustered together in the town square, Lucinda remembered they had passed a pond with some ducks on it on the edge of the town. This prompted her to buy some bread from one of the hawkers, and they paused on their way back to the carriage to toss the ducks some small chunks, watching with pleasure as the delighted birds flapped and squawked as they fought greedily over the bread.

Lucinda was momentarily distracted when two men walking towards them caught her eye. Perhaps it was because they had dark, predominantly foreign looks and seemed out of place in this quiet Yorkshire town that drew her attention. The taller of the two was thickset, while the other had sharp, weasel-like features, a hooked nose and lank hair. They were both dressed in sombre black and their swarthy complexions bespoke the Mediterranean, which made them stand out among the ordinary folk of Easterlea. As they passed by they looked directly at Lucinda, their dark eyes meeting and locking on hers, interest flickering in their depths. This brief contact, which lasted no longer than a moment, sent a strange chill down Lucinda's spine, and when they had averted their gaze and carried on, her eyes continued to follow them, watching until they had disappeared from sight.

A vague feeling of unease stole over her which she could not explain. She was curious as to their identity and strangely it brought to mind the encounter she'd had in York when she had first met Lord Rainborough and the Spanish woman with him. A frown creased her brow when she turned back to the squawking ducks, and again Amelia's chatter intruded into her thoughts. For now the incident was forced from her mind—but not forgotten.

Arriving back at the manor, they saw guests strolling in the grounds around the house. Climbing down from the carriage, Lucinda and

Amelia went inside—Lucinda having every intention of escaping to her room immediately. Lady Lampton was in the hall with a group of ladies but, on seeing Lucinda, she excused herself and broke away, moving towards them.

'So—you are back. You enjoyed your visit to Easterlea, I hope?'

'Yes, thank you, Lady Lampton. It's a lovely town,' answered Lucinda. 'Has my aunt been down yet—or is she still in her room?'

'In her room. I went in to see her earlier and she told me she would be down shortly. She promised to stroll down to the beach with me later.'

'I'll go and see if she needs anything. Please excuse me.'

'Of course, my dear, but just spare me a moment, will you?' she asked, placing a restraining hand gently on Lucinda's arm as she was about to move away with Amelia still in tow, who, believing that now she had an eager recipient for her chatter, was reluctant to be parted from her. 'My cousin has arrived and has been asking for you.'

Following Lady Lampton's gaze, Lucinda turned and looked up to the gallery to where a man, a magnificent figure, immaculate in a perfectly cut black coat, was watching her. Even at that distance she had no trouble in distinguishing the handsome features of the Earl of Rainborough, at which her heart gave a sudden leap of surprise and consternation. He smiled down at her, a slow self-assured smile, and began to advance down the stairs.

In the surrounding haze Lucinda was no longer aware of anyone save him. How positive his presence was, how tall and broad-shouldered. Colour flooded her cheeks and then drained away, for his appearance here at Easterlea was completely unexpected. She stared at him fixedly, with a strange sensation of fatality, and the tidal wave of emotions caused by his presence overwhelmed her.

For a moment she was thrown into a panic. Her first instinct upon seeing him was to turn and run, to escape from this house in which she had hoped to find a brief respite from Rainborough and his disconcerting presence, yet at the same time she was unable to move. Suddenly her visit to Easterlea had taken on a whole new aspect—for better or worse? At that moment she was so confused she knew not which—but her heart began to beat with excitement and she felt a thrill of anticipation.

Summoning all her resources, she managed to smile. 'Why, Lord Rainborough,' she said, greeting him with cool composure. 'It is indeed an extraordinary coincidence to see you at Easterlea. Or is it?'

When he was close he looked at her, his smile

barely perceptible. 'Miss Howard!' he greeted, graciously bowing his dark head slightly in acknowledgement, his magnificent eyes not leaving hers for a moment. 'Make of it what you will, but it is a pleasure to see you here. You are recovered?'

Lucinda looked at him, slightly perplexed. 'Recovered? Recovered from what?'

'Why, from the tumble you took from your horse the last time we met.'

'Oh—that. Forgive me, but for the moment I could not remember the occasion of our last meeting. Yes, I am quite recovered—although if you cast your mind back to the circumstances it was hardly a tumble,' she said defensively. 'I have to say that I am wholly surprised to see you at Easterlea, Lord Rainborough.'

'A pleasant one, I trust? Come—say you are pleased to see me?'

'I—I am,' she stammered. 'Only—I did not expect to find you here.'

'So—you thought to escape, did you?'

'Escape? Why—I'm sure I don't know what you mean, my lord. Escape from what? Your choice of word implies that I was running away. There is nothing at Rainborough I feel the need to distance myself from. I assure you that escape was the last thing on my mind when I accepted Lord and Lady Lampton's kind and generous invitation to spend a few days at

Easterlea with my aunt. We felt the sea air would benefit us both. Henrietta would have come too, but considered it best to stay with Father.'

'Of course,' he laughed, amused by the note of indignation in her voice. 'Forgive me. It was an ill-chosen word—but I am delighted you did not refuse. As for my being here—well, there is nothing unusual in that. Beatrice is my cousin, you see.' He turned to Beatrice, who was looking from one to the other with a secretive smile playing on her lips. 'My appearance seems to have surprised Miss Howard somewhat, Beatrice. Did you not tell her you were expecting me?'

'Why, no,' she responded instantly with mild surprise. 'I was under the impression that Lucinda knew. Oh, dear, how remiss of me. Do forgive me, my dear,' she said in a manner which told Lucinda that a subtle game of deception had been played. 'I had no idea. It was not my intention to withhold such information.'

'Perhaps I should be grateful to you, Beatrice,' said Laurence, his eyes gleaming wickedly as they continued to hold Lucinda's wide-eyed gaze. 'Had you told Miss Howard of my impending visit it might have caused her to return to Burntwood Hall post-haste.'

'Then for shame, cousin,' admonished Lady Lampton, her voice quizzically amused. 'For

what reason, I ask? What have you done that is
so terrible she would feel the need to? But,' she
smiled, her eyes holding Lucinda's, 'you underestimate her, for I am sure she would have done
no such thing and would be more than capable
of holding her own with you any day. I am so
sorry, Lucinda. I should have told you that my
insufferable cousin was paying us a visit.'

Lucinda looked from one to the other, at
their blank features, and at last she saw the cool
calculation—of which she had been the
object—of a game which had been played on
her innocence. There had been a subtle con-
spiracy to bring her to Easterlea—to bring her
and Lord Rainborough together, that was plain
to her now. But who had been the instigator,
and who had been a party to it? Certainly her
aunt and Lady Lampton but what of Lord
Rainborough? Was he also a party to it or had
he been as surprised to see her at Easterlea as
she was to see him?

Her instinct told her that this was not so.
When she recollected the remarks Lady
Lampton had made on her arrival—that she
already knew all about her and complimenting
her on her looks, and of her own puzzlement
concerning this—she now knew that it was not
from her aunt that she had heard these things,
but Lord Rainborough himself.

Now that she knew she felt like an absolute

fool for not suspecting from the first but, in truth, she had not believed her aunt to be capable of such subterfuge. Until she could sort out her feelings—the kind of feelings she had never had to cope with before she was bewitched, weakened and challenged by Lord Rainborough, and all these powerful emotions she had never before experienced—she was determined to remain calm, to brazen it out. Trying to ignore the dark eyes of Lord Rainborough that rested on her tight face, and his rakish grin which set her heart beating like that of a love-sick girl, knowing he was aware of her discomfiture and amused by it, she gave a faint, scarcely perceptible shrug, took a deep breath and smiled sweetly.

'I think there has been a misunderstanding, Lady Lampton, for I am baffled as to why you should think it necessary to tell me of Lord Rainborough's visit at all. It matters not one iota to me whether he is here or not. Lord Rainborough and I are neighbours and have met only occasionally. Is that not so, Lord Rainborough?'

He smiled down at her with cynical amusement. 'Our encounters may not have been frequent, but you cannot deny that they were by any means ordinary, nevertheless. I think we know and understand each other well enough.'

'Then let us hope that while you are at

Easterlea you will have the chance of becoming
better acquainted,' said Lady Lampton, eyeing
them with keen interest, for they would make a
stunning couple. It was plain they were meant for
each other. She looked at Lucinda. 'Although
it must be said that since his return from Spain
his manners are still more suited to the camp
and his regiment than to satisfy the taste of an
attractive woman. My cousin is obstinate,
Lucinda, and noted for his persistence.'

'Indeed?' Lucinda's smile challenged him.
'Then as your cousin will have gathered, Lady
Lampton, we have that in common, for I am no
less obstinate. Tell me, Lord Rainborough, are
you to remain at Easterlea long? I would have
thought your many duties at Rainborough
would have left you with little time for
socialising.'

'My estate can do without me for a short
while, Miss Howard. Besides, as both you and
my cousin are of the opinion that I am lacking
in manners,' he said, his gaze shifting appreci-
atively to the enchanting Amelia Berrisford,
still hovering beside Lucinda and for once completely at a loss for words as she gaped up at
him as though he were a Greek god, 'then to
mix with the many beautiful ladies who grace
Easterlea at this time will give me the perfect
opportunity for improving them.'

Having noticed that Amelia had caught his

attention Lucinda took her hand and drew her forward. 'Then where better to begin than right here. Allow me to present Miss Amelia Berrisford. Amelia, this is the Earl of Rainborough.'

Again she cast Laurence a triumphant, wicked smile, looking up at him obliquely. 'I'm sure you two will get on famously and find you have much in common,' she said with meaning, which was not lost on Laurence, for she was referring to the fact that Miss Berrisford was from an extremely wealthy family and Lord Rainborough in need of a wealthy wife. 'Now, please excuse me. I really must go and see if Aunt Celia is all right.'

Lady Lampton watched her go with admiration and a satisfied smile. Lucinda's reaction, when her eyes had alighted on Laurence—her expressions of disbelief, delight and wonder chasing each other across her face in quick succession, how at first she had flushed crimson and then seemed ill at ease in his presence—told her all she needed to know: Celia had been correct in her assumption that Miss Lucinda Howard had definitely fallen under Laurence's spell. When Lady Lampton turned and caught the look of total absorption on Amelia's face as she gazed up at him, she saw Lucinda was not the only one.

\* \* \*

Lucinda entered her aunt Celia's room to find her still in bed, sitting up and resting against the pillows, her hair loose about her shoulders. Her eyes were closed but she opened them as Lucinda approached the bed, smiling and patting the covers for her to come and sit beside her.

'Come and tell me what you have been doing this morning. Beatrice tells me you went into Easterlea with Amelia Berrisford. Oh, and by the way, she informed me there have been a couple of disreputable-looking characters lurking about the manor of late—beggars or gypsies, her husband suspects. He has instructed the servants to keep an extra watch so don't go wandering off alone, will you, Lucinda?'

Lucinda sat on the bed and addressed her aunt quietly, a fleeting picture of the two men she had seen in Easterlea springing to mind.

'As a matter of fact, I did see two men fitting that description in Easterlea, and Lord Lampton is probably right. They did look a bit like gypsies—but there is another matter I wish to discuss with you, Aunt Celia.'

'Oh? Then it must be important for you to look so serious.'

'Did you know Lord Rainborough would be here at Easterlea?'

Celia was surprised and slightly taken aback

by Lucinda's question and with a guilty look averted her eyes beneath her penetrating gaze.

'Why, my dear—how could I?'

'Being Lady Lampton's cousin you suspected he might be, didn't you?'

'Well—the idea did cross my mind—I cannot deny.'

'Then why did you not tell me of their relationship?'

'It did not occur to me that I should do so. And why should I? As far as I am aware you have only met Lord Rainborough on the odd occasion—and making an issue of it tells me you regard him as a little more than just a casual acquaintance—and I can see why. Lord Rainborough is a splendid, fascinating man and devilishly attractive—of the type to appeal to many a young woman's fancy. He knows what he is about, that one—I tell you that it has not escaped my notice that he has his sights set on you.'

'No, Aunt Celia. You are mistaken.'

'I may be old, dear girl, but I am not blind. I saw it in his eyes when he looked and spoke to you the day he came to Burntwood Hall—the day Henrietta took off with Hal Ingram. Whatever your father was thinking of when he offered him Henrietta I will never know. She would never have been right for him—too timid by far. Hal Ingram's more her type. Whereas you—'

'Oh? And what about me, aunt?'

'You're a different matter entirely. You have fire in your blood, Lucinda—like I had when I was your age. Oh—I wasn't always an old spinster, you know. Because I never married does not mean I led the life of a nun. I had my moments when I was your age—I can tell you.'

Lucinda stared at her in amazement for Aunt Celia had always been a rather private person, having divulged little of her earlier life.

'Aunt—you astonish me! Was there never a man you wanted to marry?'

Celia leaned her head back against the pillows and closed her eyes, a wistful smile on her lips. 'Yes, there was someone once I might have married. He was a sea captain.'

'Did you love him very much?'

She nodded. Her expression grew suddenly grave as she remembered the handsome young man she had loved so deeply and lost so tragically. 'Oh, yes,' she murmured. 'I loved him. It was the sort of love that comes only once in a lifetime—a love everyone hopes to experience but never dares to believe in.'

'What happened to him?'

'He was killed fighting the Dutch—and—well—after that no one could quite measure up to him.'

'Oh, aunt, I'm so sorry.'

She smiled and opened her eyes. 'Don't be. It was all so long ago—and, anyway—I have my memories to keep me warm now that I am old—and when your father brought you and Henrietta to live at Burntwood Hall it brought a new meaning to my lonely life.

'Oh, Lucinda,' she said, reaching out and gripping her hand. 'You are so full of the clear-cut beauty of youth. Your whole life is spread out in front of you like a glorious, rich tapestry. Enjoy it. Use it. And if Lord Rainborough is your heart's desire then hold on to him, although,' she chuckled, 'from what I know and have seen of him then you will not have to. If you are the one he wants, then I doubt he will let you go.'

'So, aunt, you contrived to bring us together?'

'Yes. Do you mind?'

Lucinda shook her head, a warm glow on her cheeks. 'No,' she replied softly. 'No, not really.'

'When I received Beatrice's invitation to spend a few days here—and her suggestion that you and Henrietta might care to come along, especially you—it seems that when she and Cedric stopped off at Rainborough on their return journey from London, Lord Rainborough specifically suggested inviting you. I confess that I did conceive of a happy notion of bringing you together,' she divulged. 'I did not tell you he was Beatrice's cousin—or that he would be here—lest you refused to come. Oh, dear. I can see you are angry with me,' she said, her eyes fixed a little uneasily on Lucinda's unsmiling, thoughtful face.

Lucinda sighed, looking deep into her aunt's eyes, and, reaching out, she clasped Celia's hand in both her own.

'No, aunt. Not really. I could not allow myself to be angry with you. One cannot be angry with someone for doing what they conceive is right.'

'Oh? Even if I was being an interfering old woman? I would scarcely blame you if you were. I know I would be at your age. But—I am not ashamed to admit that I consider you and Lord Rainborough to be right for each other—and it goes without saying, if anything should come of it, how happy it would make your father. Now,' she said beginning to throw back the bed covers, 'send Nancy in to help me dress, will you? It's high time I was up and about. I promised Beatrice a stroll down to the beach. Be off with you now, otherwise Lord Rainborough will find some other young lady to dance attendance upon.'

At her aunt's dismissal Lucinda stood up, laughing lightly. 'You are too late, aunt. I think he already has.'

'Oh?'

'Yes. The moment Amelia Berrisford clapped eyes on him, I fear she became quite besotted.'

# CHAPTER SEVEN

WHATEVER Celia's hopes had been of bringing Lucinda and Lord Rainborough closer together at Easterlea, they were dashed by the presence of the irritating Amelia Berrisford, who clung to Lord Rainborough's side like a limpet clings to the rocks on the seashore.

Lucinda watched him being followed around by this empty-headed, wide-eyed creature from Newcastle, boldly casting covetous glances in his direction, her conniving mother hovering in the background, watching her daughter with a keen eye, having cultivated in her all the feminine tricks of simpering coquetry to capture just such a man as the Earl of Rainborough.

To Lucinda, the strange thing was that Lord Rainborough did not seem to object in the slightest to the attention being showered on him; in fact, he did not seem to find Amelia at all tiresome and seemed to encourage the irritating young creature. Maybe he was flattered by her attention, for his manners where she was concerned were always impeccable. On the times when Lucinda was in his company, Amelia's mother looked quite murderous, for she resented the fact that he and Lucinda were already acquainted.

At first Lucinda was amused by it all, wondering why Lord Rainborough didn't distance himself from Amelia, but as time went by and she watched him being charming as they strolled together through the gardens, responding politely to her flirtatious behaviour, accepting his popularity gracefully, she felt an unaccustomed rush of resentment for the intimacy that had developed between them. His behaviour was so unlike him.

Why, she asked herself, if, as her aunt had told her, he had suggested to Lord and Lady Lampton that they invite her to Easterlea, did he ignore her so blatantly? Unless, of course, he was trying to make her jealous? But no, surely not. A man of Lord Rainborough's intelligence and personality would not stoop so low as to indulge in such discreditable behaviour.

However, contrary to how the situation between Amelia Berrisford and Lord Rainborough must look to Lucinda, good manners dictated that he could not ignore Miss Berrisford, however annoying he found her to be. Lucinda would have been surprised to know just how much Amelia filled him with boredom.

But, the more they were together, it was plain to see that Lord Rainborough had certainly caused a flutter in the breast of Miss

Berrisford and that she was completely infatu-ated by him. His manner towards Lucinda was always polite and considerate, though some-what reserved, which made her confused, caus-ing her to question the signals she had read emanating from him on their previous meetings, when she had been certain that he was attracted by her.

But then, she considered, she really knew nothing about him. Perhaps he had a weakness for pretty women? She had to admit that with his looks and impressive personality she could see how attracted they would be to him. He was bound to have a strong effect on any woman—especially when one was as weak and empty-headed as Amelia Berrisford. And then there was the Spanish woman he had been with in York, whose identity still remained a mystery to her. Who was she? she asked herself. And what had happened to her?

Aristocrat he might be, but if he were indeed a philanderer then she would be better off without him. Too proud to let him see that she was confused and disappointed by his behav-iour, she always schooled her features whenever they were in each other's company—although they were never alone, and she was as polite and reserved as he. If her aunt was disappointed by the way things were turning out, then she did not show it.

Sitting in the garden with her aunt among a patchwork of different-coloured blooms filling the borders, Lucinda watched Amelia and Lord Rainborough during the long golden afternoon. Amelia sat on a bench and he stood, looking down at her in the shade of some well-blown roses climbing in profusion over trellising and intoxicating them with their strong perfume.

Seeing him bend his dark head down to Amelia's upturned face, flushed almost as pink as the roses, and hear her laugh gaily at something he said, Lucinda felt a sharp flare of jealousy. She turned away angrily, telling herself it was absurd to feel jealous of this empty-headed creature, but she was and the feeling caused her to feel quite wretched and isolated. She was inclined to think that she would be glad when her aunt decided it was time for them to return to Burntwood Hall, which would be either tomorrow or the following day. But first she had the ball which Lord and Lady Lampton had arranged for that very evening to contend with.

Unable to continue observing the display of tenderness between the two, Lucinda joined a group of ladies going to the beach. Excusing herself to her aunt, who was content to remain where she was, sitting in the shade, she turned her back on them.

The bay was bathed in light and the sea a

green velvety depth, the air as soft as the flutter of a fairy's wings. The silver sun, hanging in a tranquil azure sky, cast its sparkling rays across the waters of the bay, glancing off the tips of the gently rippling waves like sharp, twinkling prisms of light. The burnt autumn colours, blanketing the hills along the coastline and beyond, dipped gently into deep gullies in secretive shades of darkness.

The sweet scents carried on the air stunned the senses and Lucinda sat on the warm sand some distance away from the group of ladies she had accompanied to the beach. She leaned her back against the rocks and closed her eyes against the searing brilliance of the sun, wishing she could also close her ears to the high-pitched sound of the ladies' shrill voices.

She listened to a stream rippling merrily over the rocks in a gully close by, its silvery clear water running and fanning out over the sand before meeting the sea. The gentle sound of the sloughing of the surf lulled her into a mood of unexpected peace and she would have drifted into a gentle slumber had a shadow not fallen across her.

She opened her eyes, having to squint in the bright glare of the sun, and when she saw the suave features of Lord Rainborough looking down at her she struggled vainly to get her thoughts into some kind of order. The memory of how she had just left him in close companionship with Amelia Berrisford was still fresh in her mind.

To Laurence, Lucinda presented a tantalising, delightful vision, a picture of grace and serenity, sitting on the sand with her eyes closed, in a gown of the palest blue with a deeper blue overskirt. But now, as she looked up at him, he saw how her mouth softened and how the violet colour of her eyes had deepened. Her creamy skin had taken on a rosy hue and her mass of fair hair was unbound, falling about her shoulders in a thick mane.

How his fingers ached to touch it, to feel its softness. He drew in a deep breath, an excess of tenderness and longing rising up inside him, wanting her more at that moment than he had before, and he meant to have her—with or without her dowry.

'So—this is where you are.'

'And what if it is?' she replied coolly. 'I came here to seek solitude, my lord, and if you were a gentleman then you would leave me in peace.'

Laurence's eyes sparkled with mischief. 'Come—you do not mean that,' he laughed, not put off by her remark. 'I wondered where you could have got to when I saw your aunt sitting alone.'

'Why? Were you looking for me? Surely you cannot have grown tired of the delectable Miss

Berrisford already?' Lucinda taunted, once again closing her eyes, trying to seem indifferent to his presence.

Laurence smiled slowly, preferring to ignore the note of sarcasm in her remark. 'May I sit down?'

'If you must,' she replied idly, drawing her skirts about her which were spread over the sand, leaning back and keeping her eyes closed as she struggled to make her face impassive and calm.

Laurence stretched out beside her, not so much sitting as lying, his long muscular body stretched sideways to face her, regardless of the sand sticking to his suit. Supporting himself on one elbow, his dark eyes looked lazily up at her from beneath hooded lids, a heavy dark brown lock spilling over his forehead. He was completely at his ease. His very nearness made Lucinda's pulses quicken, for despite the resentment she felt over his attachment to Miss Berrisford, the strength of attraction that drew her to him continued to stun and amaze her, shaking her faith in her self-knowledge as again she experienced a delicious thrill—as she always did when confronted by his masculinity.

'I was looking for you. I thought you must have come to the beach. When Miss Berrisford's mother called her away I decided to stroll down here myself—and—in answer to your question—direct as it was—no, I have not grown tired of the enchanting Miss Berrisford. Of her constant chatter, maybe, but you have to admit that she is charming and delightful to look upon.'

'That would depend on one's taste. I suppose she could be deemed passable—if somewhat silly and empty-headed,' Lucinda could not help adding, which caused Laurence to smile and Lucinda to regret her impulsive, malicious outburst, which was most unlike her, but she could not resist it.

'No doubt when she returns and finds you gone she will seek you out. But,' she sighed, seemingly unconcerned and trying to maintain an expression of impassive calm, 'I don't suppose you will mind that, will you? After all, you do seem to be quite taken with her. And I suppose you are right,' she conceded reluctantly. 'Along with her other assets, she is delightful enough to look upon.'

'Other assets?' Laurence asked, looking at her with that half-mocking expression which Lucinda was getting to know so well.

'Mmm,' she murmured, shifting herself into a more comfortable position against the hardness of the rocks. 'The fact that she is Sir Stephen Berrisford's only child—and considering his immense fortune, made from coal, as I understand it—means that when she marries she will come well endowed to her husband with worldly goods as well as with beauty which, as impoverished as you appear to be, Lord Rainborough, should suit you very well— should you consider her a suitable candidate for a wife, that is.'

Laurence looked at her incredulously before throwing back his head and laughing loudly.

'You are incredible, Miss Howard. Because I have spent a little time with Miss Berrisford does not mean I am considering her for my wife.'

'No? Then you should make it plain to her— and her mother who, I suspect, has exactly this in mind. You encourage her by the way you look at her.'

Laurence smiled, a slow, pleased smile, for he was beginning to understand the reason for Lucinda's coolness towards him. Was it possible that she was in fact jealous of the empty-headed Miss Berrisford? If so, then he was beginning to feel thankful that the attention he'd been paying her over the last twenty-four hours might not have been in vain after all.

'I look at every pretty woman that way.'

'You do? Then you must take care, my lord, else you will have more ladies vying with each other for your title than you bargained for.'

Laurence looked at her. Her eyes were very

revealing and the resentment he saw there
brought a smile to his lips.

'And what of you, Miss Howard?' he asked
in a light-hearted, casual manner, for her
answer to his question meant more to him than
she realised just then. 'Does the thought of a
title not appeal to you?'

Lucinda looked down at him sharply. He was
giving her a strange look she could not quite
fathom, his dark eyes examining her as though
looking for an answer she could not comprehend, and she felt a sudden twinge of alarm.

'Unlike Miss Berrisford, I do not look for a
title, Lord Rainborough. I have never sought
it.'

'And if one were offered to you? Would you
not find it appealing?'

Lucinda looked at him directly. 'That would
depend on the man who came with it,' she
replied tartly, beginning to struggle to get up.

'You are going?' Quickly he stood up and
taking her hand assisted her to her feet.

'Yes, I must,' she said, disengaging her hand
quickly from his grasp, for she found his touch
quite disconcerting. Lowering her eyes she
brushed the sand from her skirts. 'See—the
other ladies are returning to the house. It would
not be considered proper for me to remain here
on the beach alone with you. People would get
the wrong idea entirely—and, anyway,' she

said, lowering her gaze, 'I would not wish to ruffle Miss Berrisford's feathers by keeping you from her.'

Laurence's mouth tightened and his eyes narrowed suddenly. 'What Miss Berrisford thinks concerns me not at all,' he said in an irritated tone, his forbearance to the way she persisted in referring to the young lady beginning to wear thin. 'Now—come. If you must return to the house then I will escort you. The last thing I want is to compromise you.'

'There is no need. Stay on the beach a little while longer. I can make my own way.'

'I insist. It is easy to lose one's footing on the rocks. It would never do to injure yourself— rendering you unable to dance at the ball tonight.'

'I do not intend climbing any rocks, my lord. But seeing that you insist, then very well. You may escort me back to the house.'

It was as they climbed the steep path back to the house that Lucinda had a peculiar feeling, causing her to raise her eyes to the hill sloping up above them. What she saw made her stop suddenly and her breath catch in her throat. Suddenly she experienced a feeling as if the hills on either side were closing in on her. The two foreign-looking men that she had seen in Easterlea the previous day when she had been with Amelia, whom she had relegated to her subconscious, now resurfaced and she knew a moment's panic, for there they were, standing looking down at them, two grim, menacingly silent figures.

'Lord Rainborough—stop a moment. Look—up there. Do you see?'

Laurence paused and followed her gaze. Upon seeing the two men he stiffened, his face darkening and becoming convulsed by a violent spasm of rage. Immediately he was galvanised into action and, with an angry cry, attempted to run up the side of the hill but, hampered by the steep sides and soft crumbling ground, he knew it was futile to try and pursue them. Immediately the two men disappeared, becoming swallowed up in the thick woods crowning the brow of the hill. Cursing under his breath, Laurence returned to Lucinda.

His sudden change of mood had startled her for it was so unexpected. His features had become dark and brooding and there was a quickening to his stride as, without speaking, he took her arm in a bruising grip and continued to climb the rugged path up to the house. Only when they were in the gardens did he release his grip and look down intently at her white face, his body taut and his features tense.

Lucinda's heart was beating so fast she could scarcely speak as she stared up at him in fear and incomprehension.

'Who were those men?' she demanded. 'They looked at you as if they knew you. You do know them, don't you?'

'No,' he answered very firmly. His words were guarded and a veiled look had come over his dark eyes. 'And do not concern yourself with them. Try and forget you ever saw them. No doubt they are the gypsies Beatrice told me have been hanging about the manor for days now.'

His angry, violent reaction to the men told Lucinda they were not gypsies, that their presence denoted something far more sinister. He did know them, she was sure of it, and would have liked to have pursued the matter, but, sensing he would resent any intrusive questions, she merely sighed and turned away, sighting Amelia hurrying towards them.

'Yes—I expect you're right.'

Amelia met them with unconcealed chagrin and claimed Laurence immediately, throwing Lucinda a look of sullen resentment. Quickly Lucinda excused herself and, with an abruptness that surprised and dismayed Amelia, Laurence did likewise.

As Lucinda prepared herself for the ball that evening it was with a curious sense of foreboding, for the sinister sighting of the two men had thrown her into fearful confusion. What was

the secrecy and mystery that shrouded the Earl
of Rainborough? Contrary to his denial of
them, she was certain he knew them. But what
did they want? She was deeply disturbed by the
incident for was it possible that there could be
some connection between those men and Lord
Rainborough? Something which involved the
Spanish woman and the child she had encountered in York?

The evening was unusually warm, the air
oppressive, with all the signs of a threatening
storm. Already the faint rumble of thunder
could be heard out at sea—but Lady Lampton
was determined that it was not going to spoil
the ball after all the hard work which had gone
into arranging it, ensuring that it would be as
successful as any other which had been held at
Easterlea Manor.

The celebrated parties and balls given by
Lord and Lady Lampton were echoes of the
London social scene, helping to appease the
isolation felt by some of the gentry in the
northern provinces. Embossed invitations to all
the neighbouring gentry and aristocracy had
been sent out, requesting their presence at the
ball to be held at Easterlea Manor that evening.
It was to be a lavish and grand affair. The long
gallery on the first floor, embellished with tap-
estries and an elaborate plaster ceiling, had

been transformed into a ballroom, its oak floor gleaming bright. The orchestra was to be stationed at one end.

Leading off from the ballroom was the supper room, lit by innumerable candles which cast a golden pool of light over the buffet tables, covered with snowy white linen cloths and laden with a wide variety of foodstuffs and bottles of the finest wines. Footmen in powdered wigs with white stockings and green-and-gold satin livery hovered, ready to dance attendance on the distinguished guests. The whole house was festooned with vases and baskets bursting with a wonderful array of flowers, mainly roses in salmon pink and the deepest reds and pristine white, filling the air with their intoxicating fragrance.

It was not Lucinda's first experience of a ball. She and Henrietta had attended several on their arrival in London, where they had spent some time before coming up to Yorkshire. For this event, and on the expert advice of her Aunt Celia, she wore a dress of plain cream silk, the overskirt of a slightly deeper shade than the petticoat, tightening at the waist and caught back at the sides with pearl clasps. The sleeves were short and edged with delicate ruffles of Flemish lace. It enhanced to perfection the soft swell of her creamy breasts rising above the tightly laced stomacher which was low cut and elaborately embroidered with tiny seed pearls. Her hair was styled simply with a long unravelling ringlet and entwined with pearls.

When the distinguished guests were all assembled—the men in elegant frock coats and powdered wigs, the ladies sparkling with jewels and dressed in some of the most sumptuous, fashionable gowns Lucinda had ever seen— after being received by Lord and Lady Lampton, the evening began with a minuet danced by the hosts, and thereafter a sequence of minuets which was to be followed by a series of country dances.

Dancers whirled over the gleaming floor, the full skirts of the ladies' dresses dipping and swaying in time to the music. Lucinda had no shortage of partners although she had to repress a feeling of regret and disappointment that Lord Rainborough was not one of them. Yet she did not let this spoil her enjoyment. Just seeing so many people together enjoying themselves, the very noise of laughter, the colour, the stimulus of the music, acted like a tonic.

The evening was well under way when Lord Rainborough appeared and immediately began conversing with a group of elderly gentlemen, drawn together by their military backgrounds. They discussed the politics of the day and the subject of the utmost interest to them all, the exploits of the Duke of Marlborough and his most recent victory at the Battle of Malplaquet on the Franco-Belgian border.

It was one of the bloodiest battles of the long war with France, as once again King Louis XIV had failed in his misguided attempt to subjugate Europe by force of arms. His bid for supremacy had been put down yet again and was due, in no small measure, to the victories won by the Duke.

As the evening wore on, there was much laughter and frivolity. The next time Lucinda saw Lord Rainborough he stood alone, contenting himself with observing the dancers, seeming unwilling to join in. Used to seeing him wearing his own dark hair, Lucinda was surprised to see him wearing a full-bottomed powdered wig and looking striking in a purple velvet coat over a waistcoat and breeches of silver damask, a cravat of fringed muslin at his throat. His features were stern and there was a dark brooding look ever present in his eyes, telling her that the sighting of the two men was still very much on his mind.

There were moments when she glanced his way and caught him watching her swaying figure as she negotiated the small, intricate steps of the minuet with her partner—just one of the many fellows clamouring to dance with her. But Laurence made no attempt to approach her, to partner her in a dance—or anyone else for that

matter—not even the delectable Amelia
Berrisford, looking the picture of perfect sweetness in a cloud of curls and pale pink lace,
although somewhat down at the mouth due to
his neglect.

Later, Lucinda again looked for his tall figure
but did not see him. Beginning to feel hot after
so much dancing, feeling her slippers pinching
her feet, and with the praises of many of the
young gallants ringing in her ears, she excused
herself to her partner and went to where her
aunt was sitting with Lady Lampton and a
group of ladies. She could not help but be
aware of a certain constraint between them.
Although they knew each other well enough,
because of the splendour of the occasion their
conversation was somewhat formal and stilted.

Seeing Lucinda coming towards her, Celia
smiled, glad to see she seemed to be enjoying
herself although disappointed that Lord
Rainborough was not present.

'Come and sit with us, Lucinda. We are busy
catching up on gossip.'

'No—thank you, aunt. I'm rather warm and
quite worn out with so much dancing. I'll just
take a little stroll if you don't mind.'

'As you like, my dear.'

'My cousin has not claimed you for a dance
yet, Lucinda,' remarked Lady Lampton. 'Or, it
seems, anyone else for that matter. For the life

of me I cannot think what's the matter with him tonight—or where he's got to. He hasn't been himself all evening.'

'Maybe he's found his way into one of the card rooms, Beatrice,' suggested Celia. 'I have observed several gentlemen heading that way.'

Lady Lampton sighed deeply. 'Yes, that is what I thought—and no doubt many more before the night is out. I tremble to think how much money will have been lost before morning.'

'If the rumours which reach us of entire fortunes lost in the establishments in St James's and elsewhere are anything to go by, then plenty,' said Celia. 'Like the tolling of the graveyard bell, gambling is hardly worth the candle.'

'Then I am thankful that my cousin does not have a fortune to lose,' replied Lady Lampton with cynicism. 'But,' she said, tapping Celia's arm humorously with her closed fan, 'one never knows—for if he has indeed found his way to the card rooms, and if he is clever enough and plays his cards right, then he might even win some. Although, where he is concerned, I have to say that I believe his departure from his regiment runs deeper than I realised.'

'Why? What makes you say that?'

'Since taking up his position at Rainborough he has schooled himself to be an impersonal observer to all that is happening on the Continent, but, with all this fresh talk of Marlborough and his recent victory over the French at Malplaquet, it is bound to have affected him in some way. The army was his life and it must trouble him deeply that he no longer has any part of it. The fact that he has inherited Rainborough and the title has done nothing to soothe his departure.' She smiled at Lucinda. 'If you should see him, my dear, please tell him that I expect to dance with him before the night is out.'

With a smile Lucinda promised to do just that, before moving away and out of the ball-room into the rooms beyond where several of the guests were reclining on sofas and in chairs—men bewailing their losses at the tables and women chatting animatedly to each other and glancing across at the men, speculating on the delights of the rest of the evening while being waited on by footmen balancing glasses of refreshment on silver trays. She passed through spacious rooms elegantly carpeted and hung with crystal chandeliers until she came to one which was dimly lit and obviously not in use. Longing to remove her slippers, which hurt her feet dreadfully, she stepped inside and closed the door behind her, leaning against it for a moment before moving further into the room.

With a deep sigh she sank onto a sofa and thankfully eased off her slippers, flexing her aching toes with relief. She was about to lean against the upholstered back when suddenly she had a peculiar, unnerving feeling that she was not alone. Quickly she rose, looking across the room which was in partial darkness. At that moment a finger of lightning ripped across the night sky, bathing the room in a brilliant white light, followed by a rolling rumble of thunder. Rain began falling heavily as the storm, which had been threatening all evening, finally broke. Lucinda's breath caught in her throat, for in the stark white light she made out a figure. In another flicker of light she recognised the posture and the sharp profile of Lord Rainborough, sitting in a high-backed chair by the window, looking out.

# CHAPTER EIGHT

LUCINDA'S heart lurched uncontrollably for Lord Rainborough was the last person she had expected to find there. He sat very still, obviously deep in thought, and Lucinda was struck by his stern profile against the yellow glow from the candles. Something was troubling him, that was obvious. Something he preferred to keep to himself. Maybe Lady Lampton was right in her assumption that his departure from his regiment had affected him deeply, but Lucinda did not share her opinion, strongly suspecting that his change of mood had more to do with those men they had seen watching them climb the path from the beach earlier.

Sensing that his mind was elsewhere and that her intrusion would be unwelcome, she turned, intending to leave, but it was too late. Her very stillness in the room communicated itself to him by some sixth sense, and the soft whisper of her silk skirts as she moved towards the door, which could just be heard above the noise of the rain beating against the windows, caused him to turn his head.

'Wait,' his voice commanded, shattering the silence of the room.

With her back to him and her heart thumping madly Lucinda stopped, aware that he had risen from the chair and was slowly moving towards her. When he stood behind her she turned and looked up at his stern features, wanting to turn and run from the room, but she could only stand as if paralysed. It seemed as if his eyes never left hers which, on recognition, softened slightly.

'Why—my dear Miss Howard. So—it is you. Have you any idea how lovely you look tonight? For a moment I was half afraid you were a ghost come to haunt me,' he said with a caressing note to his voice. 'You startled me.'

'I—I'm sorry. I did not mean to.'

When another flash of lightning lit up the sky Lucinda moved towards the window, looking out and watching transfixed as the wind whipped up leaves on the ground and sent branches swaying wildly in the trees, causing torrential rain to lash with force against the windows.

Moving towards her and observing the faint smile on her lips and the deep glow in her eyes, Laurence asked softly, 'Are you not afraid of the storm?'

'No. I love storms like this. We used to have them on Barbados. I find them exhilarating.

This fury of nature forever fascinates and fills me with wonder. I could watch it all night.'

'What a strange person you are, Miss Howard. You never cease to amaze me.'

Drawn by the softness in his voice Lucinda turned her head and looked at him, a questioning look in her wide eyes, but he merely smiled crookedly.

'Tell me, why are you here?' he asked, letting his dark, amused eyes drift over her lovely face. 'Unless, of course, I am to assume you were seeking me.'

Hot colour flooded Lucinda's cheeks, for the deep resonance in his tone a moment before had almost seduced her into inertia.

'You assume too much, sir. I was merely seeking a brief respite from the dancing and did not expect to find this room occupied. I will go, for I have no wish to intrude upon your solitude.'

She turned, intending to depart, but Laurence, unable to believe his good fortune that she had found her way into his sanctuary— intentionally or not—had no mind to let her go so easily.

'There's no need to do that,' he said, at which she turned to face him once again. His expression was cynical. 'Solitude,' he sighed. 'Let us say that I too was seeking a brief respite from the heat of the ballroom—and the persistent attentions of a certain young lady.'

Lucinda smiled knowingly. 'Am I to understand that you mean Miss Berrisford?'

'The very same. Why—what's this?' he asked, indicating the slippers she held in her hands. A wicked light danced in the dark depths of his eyes as he eyed her quizzically. 'Too many young men stepping on your toes, is that it?'

'No,' she smiled. 'My slippers are too tight, that is all. I have to confess that I've been dying to take them off all evening.'

Laurence looked at her steadily. 'It's strange that you should appear now.'

'Oh? Why?'

'Because I was thinking of you.'

'I see. Then I am honoured that you should occupy your thoughts with me. What were you thinking?'

'How charming you looked on the beach earlier. Tell me, Miss Howard, do you like Easterlea?'

'Yes—very much. But then I like any place that is so close to the sea. Do you visit your cousin often?'

'No. Oh—I used to in the past but the army took up so much of my time that it changed all that. When Beatrice and Cedric called at Rainborough on their journey from London they insisted I visit them at Easterlea—and when Beatrice commands,' he said with some amusement, 'it is tantamount to a royal summons. Not having seen her or Cedric for some considerable time, it would have been an affront to refuse.'

'Affront!' exclaimed Lucinda. 'I cannot for one minute believe that would bother you.'

'No? Well, that's how it was. But—I have to confess that the very idea of spending any length of time at Easterlea surrounded by Beatrice's friends filled me with despondency—and I got to thinking that, if they were the usual mundane crowd of old whom they used to invite to their parties, then my time spent here could be enhanced by a couple of pretty faces.' His eyes gleamed wickedly. 'That was when I thought of you, Miss Howard, and your sister.'

'Oh? So it was you who asked Lady Lampton to invite us?'

'It was merely a suggestion to my cousin in the hope that a few days spent away from Burntwood Hall at this time would please you.'

'Why you should feel the need to please me baffles me, Lord Rainborough, but I thank you for the thought. Although did it not occur to you that, should I find out, it would cause me some embarrassment?'

'Embarrassment? No. That was not my intention.'

'Then it was kind of you.'

He frowned, his expression becoming ironic. 'Kind? I think not. It is a rare thing indeed that I do anything without good reason. However— if it makes you feel any better, then I will tell you that, because she's a close friend of your Aunt Celia, you were already on my cousin's list of guests. You and your sister, of course.'

'Oh—of course. And how would you have felt meeting Henrietta, my lord? After all, you were almost her betrothed.'

'I did not ask to marry your sister, Miss Howard. Do not forget that it was your father who approached me with the suggestion that a union between us could prove beneficial to us both.'

The sudden harshness of his voice startled Lucinda and caused her to ponder on the correctness of what he had said.

'You are right, of course. I agree that my father was to blame for the unfortunate affair and—thankfully, it has been happily remedied. But come, Lord Rainborough, you stray from the point. As I understand it, you came in here to escape Miss Berrisford. Well—I am sorry to be the bearer of unhappy tidings, but I must tell you that she is searching for you.'

Laurence's mouth twisted in a humourless smile. 'Then all the more reason for me to remain in here—for the truth is that I am in no mood for the frivolous girlish simperings of Miss Berrisford.'

Lucinda's lips quirked with amusement. 'With your glowing reputation as an experienced, battle-hardened soldier, my lord, surely you are not to be intimidated by a mere female. I agree that it is quite shameless the way Miss Berrisford follows you around, but you cannot blame her—after all, it is common knowledge that you are seeking a wealthy heiress,' she said, slightly taunting.

'I did overhear her mother telling Lady Skelton that because Amelia is having such a good time of it here at Easterlea then they may delay their departure for London by a few days. By the way you are constantly in each other's company, and the way she seeks you out, it is only natural that you arouse speculation among your cousin's guests, for it could be construed that you are publicly acknowledging that Miss Berrisford is suitable to all your requirements for a wife.'

Laurence's expression changed and he was looking down at her as if he had never seen her before—as if he could not gaze too long. 'They can speculate all they like—where young women of Miss Berrisford's calibre are concerned, I never allow my head to be governed by my emotions.'

He stepped closer, his dark eyes looking

directly into hers. 'But what of you, Miss Howard?' he said in a low, seductive voice. 'If you were to be seen in here—in a darkened room, alone with me—could not the same be said of you? That, like Miss Berrisford, you sought me out?' He smiled, leaving Lucinda in no doubt as to his meaning. 'At least with Miss Berrisford, the time spent in each other's company is done openly.'

Lucinda drew in a deep breath. In the dim light her tender, liquid violet eyes darkened and her face was drawn into a white cameo, her long ringlet of blond hair resting on her bare shoulder almost the same colour as she stared up at this strong virile man who was so close.

'I—I don't know what you mean,' she stammered softly, noticing how his dark brown eyes became almost black as they fastened on her face.

'Oh, come now, I think you do. I think we understand one another perfectly, don't you?'

They stood looking at each other, so close but without touching. Laurence's face was suspended over her's, mysterious in the dark shadows. His voice died away into the silence of the room, which, like him, seemed to be waiting, poised for her answer. When this was not forthcoming, he took the initiative to seek her answer by drawing her into his arms, his head descending to hers, to her lips, which were slightly parted and trembling.

He kissed her leisurely, deliberately, and Lucinda felt liquid fire shoot through her body. She did not resist his embrace and was power-less to do anything to prevent her lips from opening under his. As his arms tightened about her, in that instant their bodies melted together and she felt the hard muscles of his thighs pressed against her, causing a sweetness to flow through her veins.

Deprived of strength, she leaned against him, letting her slippers fall from her grasp. He bent her body backwards, his lips leaving hers and travelling down to the soft warm hollow of her throat where a tiny pulse was beating beneath her soft flesh. With her head flung back Lucinda gasped in sheer delight, and once again she lifted her head and his mouth covered hers.

With the noise of the storm raging outside they remained pressed together, time and place evaporating into the shadows about them. At that instant there was a sudden commotion outside the room of loud unrestrained mirth as young couples—having imbibed too much wine and seeking dark intimate places where they could be alone to experience the mysterious, sensual, bodily delights of each other, away from the jollifications of the ballroom and

prying, critical eyes of the older generation—
came closer.

Only then, as the boisterous sounds outside
the door penetrated her senses, did Lucinda
emerge from the trembling narcosis into which
Lord Rainborough's embrace and kisses had
sent her. The noise jolted her back to reality,
restoring her sanity. With a gasp she twisted
herself from his arms and stood back, staring at
him in bewilderment as the door was flung
open.

She spun round to see two young men, their
wigs awry, each holding the hands of two gig-
gling young ladies with flushed faces and eyes
wide and sparkling in anticipation. Seeing the
room already occupied they halted in the doorway. Their jaws dropped open in amazement
on recognising the dark, forbidding features of
the Earl of Rainborough. Recovering almost
instantly from the initial shock this unexpected
turn out had caused them, they did not trouble
to hide their glee, or their smirking lips, as their
eyes flickered over him and his lady with leering, knowing interest.

Lucinda flushed in an agony of shame and
embarrassment at being caught out in such a
compromising situation, while Laurence's reaction at being so rudely interrupted was one of
anger.

'Have you not the decency to knock before

you enter a room?' he admonished. 'Have you no manners at all?'

'I do beg your pardon, sir,' spluttered one of the young gentlemen, while the two young ladies tried to stifle their giggles behind their fans without success, not in the least perturbed at having disturbed them. In fact, they considered the whole situation hilarious. 'We thought the room to be unoccupied.'

'Then you thought wrong. Kindly leave us.'

Before any of them could make a move Lucinda picked up her slippers, avoiding Laurence's dark, angry gaze.

'Please—e-excuse me,' she stammered. 'I must go.'

Laurence reached out to try and stop her but it was useless. She went swiftly towards the door with as much dignity as she could muster. The four young people stood aside to let her pass, but once out of their sight, embarrassment and a sickening feeling in the pit of her stomach sped her through myriad rooms, away from the gaiety and noise of the ballroom and up the stairs to her room where she remained for the rest of the evening.

Lucinda did not see Lord Rainborough at Easterlea again. The following morning when she learned that he had returned to Rainborough first thing her feelings were confused—in fact, never had she felt so confused in her entire life. Was it relief she felt at not having to face him or regret that she would not? But in the clear light of day, the full import of what had happened between them faced her accusingly, and she shrank in perplexed embarrassment of what would happen when next they met.

She had no clear recollection of how she had got out of that room and found her way up the stairs, remembering only the angry face of Lord Rainborough as she had left him and the humiliation she had felt on hearing the unsuppressed giggles of the girls and seeing the leering expressions on the faces of their companions, who had borne witness to the passionate incident between herself and Lord Rainborough—of which the very thought brought a flush to her cheeks.

Lucinda did not doubt for a moment that, having come upon Lord Rainborough and herself in a darkened room with the door closed and locked in a passionate embrace, and their tongues already well lubricated with wine, the onlookers would be unable to keep quiet about the incident. No doubt news of it would be all over Easterlea by morning—which was confirmed by Amelia Berrisford, whom Lucinda passed whilst on her way down to breakfast the following morning and noticed that she was dressed for travelling. Amelia's expression was tight and she did not return Lucinda's smile but paused when Lucinda spoke to her.

'You are leaving Easterlea, Amelia?'

'Yes. Under the circumstances Mama thinks it best that we leave for London immediately.'

She was about to turn away but rounded on Lucinda viciously, unable to contain herself, her lovely beguiling face transfigured with malice as she faced her rival—making it clear to Lucinda that the brief camaraderie that had existed between them was over.

'This is all your doing, isn't it?' she hissed fiercely.

'Mine? But how can that be?' asked Lucinda, genuinely astonished.

'You were jealous, weren't you? Jealous because the Earl of Rainborough preferred to spend his time with me. You could not endure it. The moment you could contrive it—with scant regard for your reputation—you went looking for him.'

Lucinda's eyes opened wide at this surprise attack. 'Should that be so—and if I did have any such designs on the Earl of Rainborough— then I would not try to gain his attentions by using your devious and noticeably predatory methods, Amelia. As it is, I can assure you I did no such thing—and where the matter of my reputation is concerned, then that is entirely my own affair.'

'Oh—you need not look so horrified or so innocent. Everyone was scandalised when the sordid incident was uncovered to become the talk of everyone present at the ball. I have never felt such humiliation. You made a fool of me.'

Lucinda stiffened and her eyes narrowed angrily at what she considered to be an undeserved attack. 'Then I am sorry if you felt that,' she said tersely. 'But you are misinformed. I did not go looking for Lord Rainborough. We met quite by chance—and what happened afterwards is between myself and Lord Rainborough.'

'Then you cannot have made much of an impression on him,' Amelia scoffed haughtily.

Lucinda paled. 'What do you mean?'

'Why—it is obvious, isn't it?' she replied with a triumphant sneer. 'Lord Rainborough left Easterlea with some haste earlier—leaving you to face the music alone. Had you made any impression on him at all then he would not have done so. It would seem you scared him off.'

Seeing Lady Lampton come sweeping along the gallery she turned on her heel and flounced off, but not before Lady Lampton had heard her parting remark and, sensing the hostility between them, understood the situation at once.

'Oh, dear!' she exclaimed watching Amelia's retreating figure. 'It seems Amelia is quite put out. Pay no attention to her, my dear. Between you and me,' she said, lowering her voice to a conspiratorial whisper, 'she is furious that her nose has been pushed out of joint.'

Amelia's unprovoked attack was forgotten in the light of what she had told Lucinda. 'Is it true, Lady Lampton? Has Lord Rainborough left Easterlea?'

The sudden break in Lucinda's voice and her crestfallen face brought Lady Lampton's observant eyes upon her. 'Yes. At first light. But,' she said, smiling softly and patting her arm with understanding, 'you may rest assured that it had nothing to do with you—or what happened last night.'

Lucinda felt the blood fly to her face in sudden embarrassment. 'You—you know about that?'

'Yes—as does everyone else,' she laughed. 'Pay no notice. Had it not been my illustrious cousin they had come upon, locked in a passionate embrace with a beautiful young woman, then the matter would not have been worth a mention.'

'But nothing happened, Lady Lampton— well,' she murmured, lowering her gaze, know-

ing she must look the picture of guilt to Lady
Lampton, who was eyeing her with amused
suspicion, 'not really.'

'I believe you, Lucinda. My cousin is too
much of a gentleman for anything else. You
must think nothing of it.'

Think nothing of it? How could she not think
of it? What had happened in that room between
her and Lord Rainborough would remain with
her till her dying day. How could she forget
how she had felt? How it had felt to have his
arms about her, to feel his lips on hers, and how
shamelessly, wantonly, even, her own traitorous
body had responded so eagerly, betraying any
resistance she had built up against him, making
her forget so easily that she had no intention of
becoming involved with any man who saw her
as little more than a means of financially securing his future.

Aware of the turmoil going on inside her,
Lady Lampton took her arm. 'Spare me a
moment, will you, Lucinda? Let's take a turn
about the garden while it is quiet.'

Lady Lampton's expression was perfectly
natural but Lucinda was assailed by discomfort.
'Of course,' she replied, and then added as if it
were some kind of protection, 'although I
mustn't be away for too long. Aunt Celia will
be needing me.'

'Don't worry. We'll just take a stroll, that is all. How is Celia this morning?'

'Tired after so much excitement and staying up so late.'

'That's only to be expected, but I do believe she enjoyed herself.'

The morning had dawned bright and clear, with little sign of the storm which had raged throughout the night, apart from several broken branches and a few ravaged flower beds. It was quiet strolling along the paths. The gardens were noticeably devoid of people, many of the guests having risen late and still in the breakfast room. Two gardeners going about their work bade them a cheery good morning. Lucinda was thinking of Lord Rainborough. Why had he left Easterlea in such haste? Did he regret what had happened between them? Lady Lampton had tried to reassure her that it had nothing to do with her—but if not then what could it be? Once again she had a mental picture of the two men they had seen on their way from the beach. Could they have anything to do with his departure?

'Why did Lord Rainborough have to leave?' she asked suddenly.

'A letter arrived from Rainborough. As to its contents I know not—but one thing I do know is that it must have been urgent for him to take off like that.'

They walked on for a few moments in silence before Lady Lampton continued, studying the serious expression on Lucinda's face with understanding, sensing some of the puzzlement she must be feeling over Laurence's behaviour.

'I can see that you have formed quite an attachment for my cousin, Lucinda.'

Lucinda paused, unable to look into Lady Lampton's eyes directly, for she had an alarming way of reading the truth. 'No—at least not in the way you mean, Lady Lampton. As I said—we scarcely know one another.'

Laughing softly at Lucinda's sudden confusion, unconvinced by her reply, Lady Lampton put her hand under her chin and turned her face up to hers. 'One doesn't have to know someone well to fall in love, you know. Attachments of that kind are often made at first glance. That is how you feel, isn't it?'

Taken by surprise by Lady Lampton's frank speaking, Lucinda flushed. Love! What did she know of love? She had never been in love so how could she know what it was like? Was it the sudden quickening of excitement inside and the way one's eyes were irresistibly drawn to someone else's? She was strongly attracted to Lord Rainborough—this she was aware of, and whenever they were together he had a strong, pulsating effect on her. But *love*? How could she answer Lady Lampton?

'Perhaps if you had used your charms on him, flirted with him a little, then more of his time would have been spent with you instead of Amelia,' Lady Lampton said gently. 'Amelia is a delightful girl and her mother and I have been friends for many years. She is an only daughter and her parents mean for her to marry well. To capture an earl would have been a grand-sized feather in their cap indeed.'

Stiffened by pride, for she was slightly offended by Lady Lampton's suggestion that she should have behaved in the same frivolous, immature manner as Amelia Berrisford had done, Lucinda's expression became tight.

'Yes—I can see that it would. However—I am quite inexperienced in the employment of such frivolous arts, Lady Lampton, and find little joy in engaging in meaningless flirtations merely to capture a gentleman's attention.'

Lady Lampton's dark eyes appraised her with admiration and understanding. 'So I am beginning to realise. You are far too intelligent for that and Laurence is much too serious to play fast and loose. I know him well, Lucinda, and I was not taken in for one moment by the attentions he bestowed on Amelia. He was quite indifferent to her charms, however it may have looked. But nor am I so blind that I cannot see for myself where his true affections lie—

especially when I heard what occurred between you last night.'

'I think that can be explained, Lady Lampton. I believe Lord Rainborough got quite carried away by the moment, for normally I would say he is not interested in me but in a very different matter which concerns my fortune.'

'With your fortune you are a desirable asset, I agree, and it cannot be easy for Laurence with a rundown estate to maintain. He knows what has to be done—what it will cost—and the sensible solution is for him to marry an heiress. This he can do while ever his heart remains unattached. But this I do know about my cousin, Lucinda—that if he meets a woman and falls deeply in love with her, then all the money in the world would be of no consequence whatsoever to that.'

Beginning to feel slightly disturbed by this conversation she was having with Lady Lampton, unsure as to where it was leading, Lucinda averted her eyes and began to walk on slowly, Lady Lampton falling into step beside her.

'You say you know Lord Rainborough well, Lady Lampton. Are you his cousin on his mother's side?'

'Yes. Laurence's mother and my own were sisters,' she explained. 'He was an only child.

We spent a good deal of time together as children at his home on the outskirts of York—and I have to say that when his parents died he was still only a boy. From then on—when he was not at Oxford finishing his education—he lived at Rainborough with his uncle and Rupert until he took up his commission, making the army his life. The death of his uncle, followed so soon by that of Rupert, making him sole heir to the Rainborough estate, hit him hard. Family honour and duty were paramount to all else. As he saw it, he had no choice but to resign his commission. He has a lot to learn about living his life away from the army.'

Lucinda paused and looked seriously at Lady Lampton. 'Why are you telling me this, Lady Lampton? Lord Rainborough and I live but a short distance from each other. At this moment we are acquaintances, nothing more. Why should you think any of this has anything to do with me?'

'Because Laurence is much taken with you—I do know that. In fact, to tell the truth, Laurence would not have asked me to invite you to Easterlea if it were otherwise. He is meticulous about such matters and would not, I know, put forward such a request if he were not serious. He also told me that you were the most beautiful girl he has ever met—and Laurence does not eulogise lightly.'

'He—he said that?' stammered Lucinda, her eyes open wide in astonishment. 'But—I cannot credit it.'

'Ah—but it is true. I agree with him. You are lovely, my dear.'

Not wishing to add to Lucinda's confusion, or make it look as if she were matchmaking, Lady Lampton did not add that as far as she was concerned Laurence needed a wife and Rainborough a mistress—the sooner the better—and that she would be delighted if he chose Lucinda whom she was sure would prove more than capable of taking on both, for she was intelligent and did not lack either sense or spirit. Yes—she would suit Laurence very well.

'For too long Laurence has had little time to include love in his life,' she continued, 'but that does not mean to say that ladies don't live in hope,' she laughed. 'I well remember the times—before the army instilled into him the discipline necessary to make a good soldier— when he wasn't so stiff and formal and used to enjoy the gaieties of the London season as much as the rest.

'When he came home from the Continent from some campaign or other, his good looks and the fact that he was a soldier—a hero, even, and thought highly of by the Duke of Marlborough himself—made him an extremely popular figure indeed. Women were forever at his heels. But,' she frowned, her dark eyes suddenly troubled, 'he has changed a great deal from those days. Oh—it isn't just his departure from the army that has brought this about. He has changed in other ways, too.'

'What do you mean, Lady Lampton?'

'Laurence and I have always been close but he does not always confide in me. Since he returned from Spain there is an air of secrecy about him—something mysterious that worries him. Something happened over there which has affected him deeply—I am certain of it. It is something he will not speak of.'

Lucinda stared at her with interest, for she had just voiced her own thoughts. These same suspicions were foremost in her own mind.

Lady Lampton looked at her intently. 'Do you know what it might be, Lucinda? Has he said anything at all to you?'

'No. But then, if he hasn't confided in you he certainly wouldn't confide in me. I have told you—we scarcely know each other.'

Lucinda had to admit that what Lady Lampton had said was true. An air of mystery did surround Lord Rainborough, but if he had wanted his cousin to know the cause of it, then surely he would have mentioned it. The fact that he hadn't probably meant the matter was serious and he did not wish to give her cause to worry.

But ever since Lucinda had first become acquainted with Lord Rainborough—since she had seen him in York with the young Spanish woman and the child—she had been curious about him, her curiosity increasing on the arrival on the scene of the two foreign-looking men, causing him to react to their appearance violently. And now there was the note that had been delivered to him in the early hours from Rainborough. What could it have contained to make him leave Easterlea in such haste? Were all these incidents connected?

Lucinda did not divulge any of what she already knew to Lady Lampton, feeling it was not her place to do so and not wishing to increase her worry. No doubt if there was cause for her to be concerned then Lord Rainborough would sort it all out eventually and put her mind at rest—but until such a time she would keep her own counsel.

'I think that maybe you worry needlessly, Lady Lampton. It is inevitable that Lord Rainborough's transition from the strict disciplines of army life to that of running an estate on such a large scale as Rainborough was bound to have had some effect on him.'

Lady Lampton sighed, knowing Lucinda was trying to soothe her anxiety where her cousin was concerned? and she smiled gratefully, but she was not mollified. She smiled resignedly.

'Yes—I am sure you're right. I do recognise the difficulties he must face and think, perhaps, I'm being a little over-protective—which will never do. Come—let us head back to the house. Oh—see—at last,' she laughed suddenly on observing a number of guests beginning to wander out of the house. 'After sleeping off their excesses of the ball, I am glad to see our guests are beginning to stir at last.'

# CHAPTER NINE

LAURENCE hurried to York faster than he had ever hurried anywhere in his life before, mastering his impatience to spur the horses on. The closer he got, desperation, born out of pure fury, drove him on, but resisting the overwhelming urge to leap out of the coach and take the reins from the driver and drive the horses himself in his desire to reach his daughter before it was too late.

Darkness had long since fallen by the time they crossed Monk Bridge which spanned the River Foss outside the ancient city. He had been on the road since early morning, having left Easterlea immediately he had received the note from William telling him that word had arrived at Rainborough Castle from Anthony Metcalfe and his wife in York, that his daughter was very sick and he must go to her at once.

Laurence breathed a sigh of relief when the coach finally passed through Monk Bar, the tallest of the four gates which pierced York's two-and-a-half-mile defensive circle of creamy limestone wall. Expertly the coach driver negotiated the way through the city, interconnected

by narrow lanes between tightly-grouped, centuries-old houses, towards Micklegate. Thankfully few people were abroad, the streets devoid
of the congestion of wagons and people which
prevailed during the day time, when the journey
within the city walls would have seemed
interminable.

After travelling down Ouse Gate, they
crossed the humped-backed Ouse Bridge, the
only crossing over the river apart from the ferry
upstream near Barker Tower. The coach
climbed the steep incline of the bridge's central
bow and down the other side, passing St
William's Chapel on the Micklegate end of the
bridge with its distinctive needle spire. Across
from it stood the most foul and dampest of
York's gaols, where during daylight hours—
which lasted only until noon in its lower parts—
prisoners were in the habit of begging food
from passers-by.

After passing the Priory of the Holy Trinity
along Micklegate, it was with abject relief that
Laurence saw Metcalfe Hall ahead—a large
timber-framed, two-storey house with three
gables and jettied tiled roof. It had elaborate,
wooden, gothic windows and spandrels forming
a handsome porch facing the street. The coach
passed through an arched gateway into a cobbled yard. Metcalfe Hall was the home of
Anthony and Margaret Metcalfe, whom

Laurence had known since boyhood. The three of them had grown up together when Laurence had lived along The Mount, which was outside York on the Tadcaster road. The three of them had remained close over the years and it had been a happy day when Anthony and Margaret had married. Unlike Laurence, who had been determined to make his career with the army, Anthony had entered his family's law firm, practicing in York.

On his return from Spain, and owing to events which had occurred in that country making it almost impossible for him to take his three-year old daughter to Rainborough Castle—and not knowing how run down and neglected he would find things there—it was to Metcalfe Hall that Laurence had brought her, for Anthony and Margaret to care of until such a time when he could safely take her home.

The moment the coach pulled into the yard and Laurence climbed out, Anthony was there to meet him. He was a man of medium height with a broad frame and blue, quizzical eyes which took in his friend's appearance at once, causing him to wince at the haggard set of his face and the tortured look in his dark eyes.

'Praise be to God you are here at last, Laurence.'

'I came as quickly as I could. Unfortunately, when word arrived at Rainborough I was over half a day's journey away visiting my cousin at Easterlea. How ill is Christina?'

'She has the scarlet sickness, Laurence. We considered it best to send for you when her condition deteriorated for we feared the worst. Mercifully, her fever broke last night. The news is hopeful.'

'Thank God—but how I wish I could have been with her during those critical hours.'

'Come along inside. Some refreshment, per-haps—but first I will take you to Christina.'

They were met on the landing by Anthony's wife Margaret. She was carrying a pitcher of water which she placed on a table on seeing Laurence, smiling suddenly and moving for-ward to greet him. Margaret was as tall as her husband, a quiet, attractive young woman with a graceful bearing, auburn hair and intelligent brown eyes.

'Laurence! How good it is to see you at last.'

'I was telling Anthony that I came just as soon as I received word, Margaret.'

'I'm sure you did. Come along inside. No doubt you're anxious to see Christina.'

Laurence entered the chamber where his daughter slept, the light from the candles and the fire glowing rich in the heat, bathing the room in a gentle glowing warmth. The still figure of Maria, Christina's Spanish nurse, sat outside the circle of light, her eyes lowered and her lips moving in silent prayer as her fingers passed over the beads of her rosary threaded through her fingers. When Laurence entered the room she lifted her head, her eyes flooding with relief at the sight of his familiar figure.

Laurence looked down at the frail, helpless child in the bed, his throat constricting with pain when he thought he had almost lost her to the Almighty. Sitting beside her, he gently took one of her small limp hands in his, finding it hard to imagine that this exhausted child was the same warm, vital sprite he had left behind with Margaret and Anthony when he had gone to Rainborough. Golden candlelight touched her cheeks and her dark-lashed eyes were closed as she slept, her face, smattered with scarlet dots, pale now the fever had gone, her pallor emphasised by the whiteness of the lace-trimmed pillow on which she rested her head. She was so small that the huge four-poster bed, hung with heavy azure brocade, almost swallowed her up.

Margaret came to stand beside him, looking down.

'She has been fretting for you, Laurence,' she said quietly. 'Last night her fever broke and now she does not cry out or toss so much. The doctor says the danger is past, that she is over the worst. He has great hopes for her recovery. The rash will fade gradually.'

Realising the tremendous strain he must have been under since learning of Christina's illness, she smiled softly, observing how his shoulders relaxed at her words and the tension seemed to melt from his face when he looked up at her questioningly.

'She's going to be all right, Laurence. She's going to get better. Now—come and take some refreshment. You look quite worn out. You can sit with her later.' Her eyes moved fondly to where Maria still sat. 'Perhaps now you are here, Maria can be persuaded to take some rest. She has watched and nursed Christina constantly, afraid to take her eyes from her for one moment. Her devotion to the child is commendable.'

Leaning over, Laurence touched Christina's cool brow with his lips before rising and following Margaret from the room. Downstairs she disappeared to the kitchen to arrange for refreshments to be brought for their guest, leaving Laurence alone in the drawing-room with her husband, who handed him a much-needed glass of Madeira.

The strong fortified wine flowing through his veins helped to relieve the tension inside him, and he felt his body begin to relax. Moving towards the fireplace where a fire blazed in the iron grate, he gazed down into the flames, realising how precious his lovely, beautiful child was to him, how close he had come to losing her. He marvelled at her resilience, while the full horror of what her loss would mean to him entered his soul.

Gazing at his friend's brooding face, Anthony moved to stand beside him.

'Christina will soon be well enough for you to take to Rainborough as planned, Laurence.'

'I cannot take her yet, Anthony. It is not possible.' He sighed with a weariness he had not felt in a long time. 'I am beset on all sides. Everything is in such a mess at Rainborough and I am absent for most of the time—overseeing what has to be done on the estate myself for the present. There would be no one to take care of her except William and my elderly housekeeper. I want a more settled environment to take her back to. You do understand that, don't you?'

'Of course. In any case, she will not be well enough to travel for some considerable time. Margaret and I are more than happy for her to remain with us for just as long as it is necessary. You know that. With no child of our own as yet, Margaret positively dotes on her. I am only sorry we had to send for you. Others have gone down with the same ailment but have not been as fortunate as Christina.'

Laurence turned and looked at him. 'Words cannot express my gratitude, Anthony, to you and to Margaret for sheltering her—taking care of her—but you know the other reason why I cannot take her back to Rainborough, why her whereabouts must be shrouded in secrecy.'

Anthony nodded grimly, remembering what Laurence had told him of his time in Spain, how he had been caught in a compromising situation with a young Spanish girl, Isabella de Silva. Unbeknown to him, she was of noble descent and, upon discovering the relationship, her father, Don Philippe de Silva, had been incensed with rage. Accusing him of disgracing his daughter, he had ordered them to marry. Laurence had done the honourable thing and married her but his duties with his regiment had kept them apart. Their union had been brief and Isabella had borne him a daughter, Christina, before dying shortly after the birth.

When Laurence had left Spain he had brought his daughter and her nurse Maria with him. His action had brought strong opposition from her grandfather who, feeling cheated and heartbroken over the death of his beloved daughter, had wanted to keep the child. When Laurence had insisted on taking her, as was his right as her father, Don Philippe had sworn to hunt him down and get the child back.

In his native Cadiz, Don Philippe was a powerful man and Laurence did not doubt for one moment that he would do his utmost to carry out his threat and track him down in England. Not knowing what awaited him at Rainborough Castle, and with this fear in mind, he had asked Anthony and his wife to take care of her for the time being.

'Already I have reason to suspect that my worst fears have been realised—that Don Philippe has sent men to England in an attempt to abduct Christina,' explained Laurence gravely. 'Two men—one I am certain I have seen before in Spain—are watching me. I saw them at Easterlea only yesterday and pray to God they did not follow me here.'

'Is it possible?'

'There is a chance.'

'Then we will see to it that she does not leave the house. Fear not, we will take good care of her. Now—tell me—have you given any more thought to Sir Thomas Howard's proposal that you marry his daughter?'

Laurence shook his head wearily. 'Miss Henrietta Howard was not enamoured of the idea of marriage to me. She wept and lamented woefully at the very thought. It seems her heart was already elsewhere. Sir Thomas has conceded to her wishes and, from what I understand, she is to wed quite soon.'

'Then I am sorry to hear it.'

Laurence shrugged and smiled slowly, a softness entering his dark eyes when Lucinda's image floated in his mind. 'There is no need. It is of no matter to me. In fact, I was rather relieved, I can tell you.'

'Ah!' Anthony exclaimed, his interest aroused, for the tone of his voice and the secretive smile hovering on his lips led him to believe there might be good reason for his apparent unconcerned reaction to Miss Henrietta Howard's rejection. 'I see.'

'You do?'

'Aye,' he chuckled. 'More than you realise. Tell me—who is the fortunate lady who has captured your interest?'

'Henrietta's sister. Miss Lucinda Howard.'

'You speak her name like a term of endearment. Does she resemble her sister?'

'A little—but her character is so very different,' said Laurence, thinking with pleasure of the previous evening—of the ball at Easterlea and what had transpired between them when they had found themselves alone. He remembered how it had felt to hold her, how warm she was in his arms, how supple, how willingly she had yielded her lips, opening them to receive his kiss.

He sighed, swallowing what remained of the Madeira in his glass as he also remembered the shock and embarrassment in her eyes when they had been so rudely interrupted, how she had turned from him and hurried from the room, horrified that their passionate interlude had been witnessed by others who had derived immense pleasure in their discomfort. Did she regret her moment of weakness when she had surrendered to his embrace? And what had she thought when she had found he had left Easterlea so suddenly?

'Henrietta is meek and demure,' he continued, 'and does not possess the same vibrant qualities I find attractive and challenging in her sister. Lucinda is stubborn and forthright with fire in her blood and a rebellious heart.'

'Then mayhap her rebellious heart will be chastened with marriage, Laurence,' smiled Anthony. 'At least marriage to her would bring you the much-needed wealth to restore Rainborough.'

'Aye—that I know. But had she no dowry at all, I would marry her.'

'And what does the fair Lucinda think of you, Laurence? Does the prospect of being a countess appeal to her feminine heart?'

'Not in the slightest. She will not be swayed by prospects of grandeur. She thinks little of marriages arranged like commercial transactions for the acquisition of wealth, lands or power.'

'Then she is a rarity indeed.'

'Her dowry would be a desirable asset—that I am in no position to deny. Rainborough desperately needs a fortune spending on it to survive. But how can I convince her that I would marry her for herself and not what she will bring? That I would live in poverty for the rest of my life just to have her by my side.'

Anthony gave him a laughing sidelong look. 'From what I remember of you, Laurence, you never had any problems in that quarter. However—there is only one way of finding out whether she will have you or not and that is to ask her—for the sooner you are married and some semblance of order has been restored to Rainborough then the sooner you will be able to take Christina there. Does Miss Lucinda Howard know you have a daughter?'

'No. Apart from her father, no one does. As a prospective husband for his daughter, he had a right to know my circumstances, but until I am able to take Christina to Rainborough— when I am certain she will be safe from abduction by her grandfather—then I asked for his silence. The fewer people who know of her existence the better. I want no word uttered in idle gossip to lure any would-be kidnappers to her whereabouts. I would only have revealed her existence to Henrietta if she had considered marriage to myself favourable.'

'And should you decide to ask her sister instead? How do you think she will take the disclosure that you have a daughter? Do you think she will be willing to take on the responsibility of a child?'

'That I cannot say. But if I am to propose marriage then it is a chance I shall have to take.'

Lucinda was unusually quiet on the return journey to Burntwood Hall as she pondered over the conversation she'd had earlier with Lady Lampton in the garden, causing her curiosity over Lord Rainborough to deepen. What was the mystery all about that caused his cousin to be so concerned? She sighed, staring out of the coach, passing scenery which became a blur for she wasn't really seeing any of it.

Her short visit to Easterlea had certainly proved to be eventful — not in the least like she had expected. Where was Lord Rainborough now? she wondered. Why had he left so suddenly and without a word to anyone, leaving her to face the humiliation and whisperings at Easterlea alone? When would she see him again? And when they did meet how would things be between them? At the thought of coming face to face with him again after their shared, intimate moment, a soft, embarrassed flush mantled her cheeks and a nervous feeling of excited pleasure stole over her.

For the time it took to travel from Easterlea to Burntwood Hall, which took two hours

longer than their outward journey owing to the
wet and rutted condition of the roads caused by
the recent rain, Celia dozed, saying little. She
had been made aware by more than one of
Beatrice's guests, eager to relate what had
transpired between Lucinda and Lord
Rainborough the previous evening, and she was
neither shocked nor dismayed by it—in fact,
she was rather pleased by the way events were
turning out.

Clearly Lucinda was troubled and confused
by what had occurred so Celia remained quiet
on the subject, but her eyes were watchful, their
powers of discernment sharp, for she had a
strong suspicion that it would not be long
before Lord Rainborough paid Thomas a call
at Burntwood Hall, requesting his permission
to marry Lucinda. On this happy thought she
sighed and closed her eyes, leaning her head
against the soft upholstery as the coach rumbled
along.

On arriving back at Burntwood Hall it was to
find Henrietta in a state of euphoria, for her
father had relented in all things where Hal was
concerned. Not only had he become a frequent
visitor to the house but Sir Thomas also gave
the happy couple his blessing, permitting their
marriage to take place just as soon as it could
be arranged. There was no sense in waiting and

he was eager for it to take place soon owing to his own failing health.

Hal Ingram was a nice-looking, sensible young man—though in Lucinda's opinion a trifle dull. He always appeared rather awkward, his speech slightly hesitant and he had an apologetic manner—due, she suspected, to the fact that he lived in the shadow of his domineering father and notorious brothers, well known for their disreputable, unrestrained behaviour in the district.

She wondered what they thought about Hal's impending marriage to Henrietta. No doubt they would be rubbing their hands in glee, already itching to grasp some of the wealth that would come his way. Fortunately, both her father and Aunt Celia were astute business people and would know what they were about. With the help of their lawyer, they would be very careful to draw up a settlement, making certain not a penny of Henrietta's dowry found its way into their grasping hands.

Lucinda did not see Lord Rainborough for several weeks, nor did she hear any news of him. She did not know where he was or, indeed, if she would ever see him again. But she did miss him terribly—more than she dared admit to herself, for her feelings where he was concerned filled her with confusion. Whether or

not he had returned to Rainborough Castle she
had no way of knowing. Often she was tempted
to call for the carriage and visit Rainborough
Castle, but her pride prevented her from doing
so or asking questions.

Doubts began to cloud her mind and she was
bitterly wounded by his treatment of her. She
had been so sure he had been attracted by
her—aware of her physically—and his conversation had led her to believe that he was leading
up to something. Clearly she had been mistaken. Never would she trust her own instincts
again.

Had the kiss that had woken all the passionate desires inside her meant nothing to him
after all? Finding life dull in this quiet rural part
of Yorkshire, had he merely been playing with
her affections for want of something better,
more exciting, to do? She'd heard of men taking
advantage of innocent young ladies and then
leaving them without the slightest remorse. But,
no, she told herself, Lord Rainborough wasn't
like that. Hadn't Lady Lampton told her it was
not in his nature to play fast and loose?

She tried telling herself that his absence did
not concern her one way or the other, that she
could be as dispassionate as he was—but if this
was truly the case, then why did it hurt so
much?

The house was a-buzz with wedding preparations and Lucinda was grateful to have plenty to do to keep her busy and her mind occupied. But it was at night when Lord Rainborough's image invaded her dreams, when he was seldom out of her thoughts. She didn't sleep well, tossing and turning night after night, remembering the feel of his caress and his lips on hers.

The day of the wedding finally arrived, a cold but bright November day. It was a simple, quiet affair—Sir Thomas being too ill to withstand too much excitement. There were few guests and the ceremony was performed in the Norman church in the centre of Rainborough. Afterwards, a small reception was held at Burntwood Hall for the guests where everyone wished the happy couple well. Henrietta, all silk, ribbons and lace, looked radiant and gazed with pride and joy at Hal, telling Lucinda that it was the happiest day of her life.

A week later, when the household had returned to normal—and with the addition of another person to the family—just when Lucinda had almost convinced herself that what had passed between herself and Lord Rainborough had meant nothing to him after all, feeling angry that he had found it so easy to dismiss her from his life, she returned from riding one afternoon to discover that this was

not so, for while she had been absent he had
called at Burntwood Hall.

Lucinda went into the drawing-room where
her aunt was waiting to speak to her. The
meeting with Lord Rainborough had taxed her
father's strength and he had retired to his room.
Following the upheaval of Henrietta's wedding,
Celia was tired and would have liked to have
done the same but she waited for Lucinda to
return from her ride, hoping that what she had
to tell her would dispel the look of misery in
her eyes which had been present ever since
their return from Easterlea.

She had been wan and listless, unable to hide
her unhappiness brought about by Lord
Rainborough's absence and failure to commu-
nicate, no matter how hard she tried. Celia
looked at Lucinda directly, wondering how she
would react to his reason for coming to
Burntwood Hall today.

'You wanted to see me, aunt?'

'Yes. Lord Rainborough called, Lucinda. He
has asked for your hand in marriage.'

Lucinda became still, her eyes fixed on her
aunt. If this proposal had come soon after her
visit to Easterlea then it would have come as no
surprise—in fact, she had been half expecting
it, but now, after the multitude of doubts which
had plagued her of late, it had come as something of a shock to her sensibilities. Her face

became drained of colour but, apart from that, her expression remained blank.

'I see. What did you tell him?'

'That we would speak to you, of course.'

'Could he not ask me himself?'

'You were not here, Lucinda. And, anyway— it was only right that he should seek permission to do so from your father first. However, he is to call again when you have had time to consider the matter.'

'How generous of Lord Rainborough,' Lucinda replied, her reply unusually testy. 'What is it to be? One week? Two weeks? How long is it before the bills have to be paid at Rainborough?'

'Lucinda,' reproached her aunt. 'That is hardly fair—and it is not like you to be so outspoken.'

'Nevertheless, I strongly suspect that is the way of things, aunt. I am not so naïve as to see that he would not have proposed had my father not settled on me a generous dowry—that, should we wed, I will drop a fortune at his feet.'

'Your dowry will be quite substantial, of course.'

'Of course. If it were not, I very much suspect he would look for a wife elsewhere.'

A pained look entered Celia's eyes at this reaction to what she had hoped would be a reason for rejoicing. 'You do Lord

Rainborough an injustice, Lucinda. He is not as mercenary as you make him out to be.'

'I don't.'

'Yes, you do. I know what happened between the two of you at Easterlea and I know that his hasty departure without a word to anyone and his silence since then have hurt and angered you deeply. But he had good reason for leaving in the manner he did.'

Lucinda looked at her sharply. 'You know? He told you?'

'Yes. But it is not my place to divulge to you what he told your father and me in confidence. I believe he would prefer to do that himself.'

Lucinda took in a deep breath, digesting her Aunt Celia's words. 'I see.'

'Lord Rainborough cares for you deeply, Lucinda. I am sure of it.'

'Even without my dowry, Aunt Celia?'

'Forget your dowry,' snapped Celia, sounding unusually harsh, giving Lucinda an unsympathetic look, 'and have the courage to take things as they are. Good heavens! What is the man supposed to do? Can he help it if his cousin died, leaving Rainborough in such a ruinous state? He gave up a great deal when he relinquished his career in the army. Out of a sense of duty and loyalty to his forebears and future generations of Dwyers he is determined to do his utmost to preserve intact the noble house of

Rainborough. He is a proud and honourable man, Lucinda—and will dislike the terms of the marriage contract as much as you. But I sincerely believe that such is his devotion to you he would wed you without the fortune you will bring—should you accept his proposal of marriage.' She sighed and when she spoke again her tone was less severe. 'Think how happy you could be living at Rainborough, Lucinda. It's a wonderful place. You will consider Lord Rainborough's proposal seriously, won't you?'

Lucinda had the grace to look slightly abashed. 'Yes,' she whispered. 'Of course I will.'

'Goodness—you'll be Countess of Rainborough—with your own castle and manor and a husband who will love you. It will be a far cry indeed from Barbados.'

Where lies the beauty of the old days and the innocence of my lost childhood, thought Lucinda wistfully, and her heart ached with a sad hunger for them to return. But what was the use of wanting them to return? Of looking back? Those days were gone now, sweet memories gone for ever. They were nothing to her now.

Now she must look to the future. Aunt Celia was right. She could be happy living at Rainborough and she did understand, having seen the castle for herself, Lord Rainborough's own deep love for the place, how he could not bear to part with it. She would have done exactly the same in his situation and gone to any lengths to hold on to it—even if it had meant marrying an heiress.

# CHAPTER TEN

LORD RAINBOROUGH gave Lucinda one week
to consider his proposal of marriage. When
Celia told her that he had arrived at Burntwood
Hall and awaited her in the drawing-room, she
was overcome with relief and a strange light-
heartedness, her fears and uncertainties vanish-
ing like the morning mist. She paused before
entering the room, taking a tentative step towards
the closed door, for it was more difficult than
she had anticipated. So much time had elapsed
since their last meeting—the events of that meeting—of their embrace and how she had fled from
him, still vividly clear in her mind. Nervously
she entered the room. Seeing him, a wave of
happiness swept over her, making her forget the
doubts that had assailed her during his absence,
driving out the anxieties of the past weeks.

He was dressed immaculately in plain black,
the whiteness of his stock emphasising his dark,
lean features which were drawn and lines of
worry and fatigue creased his brow. Grave
matters clearly worried him which deepened
Lucinda's curiosity as to where he had been for
the past weeks.

Laurence watched her enter the room and move gracefully towards him. His gaze slid slowly over her face. He inclined his head towards her, feeling an instant response to her beauty, her femininity, seeing how the sunlight lit up her hair like a silken sheath as she passed the window. He studied her with a degree of intensity, observing her pallor and the dark shadows beneath her eyes.

'I am delighted to see you again after so much time—although I must say you are look-ing pale. You have not been ill, I hope?'

'No, thank you for your concern. I am quite well. If I am pale, then it can only be put down to the upheaval of Henrietta's wedding. It has been quite chaotic for some time. Only now has some semblance of order been restored to the household.'

Laurence's lips curved in a crooked smile and there was amusement in his voice. 'I see. And here was I thinking the reason might be because you have missed me.'

'Why, no,' she lied, lowering her gaze lest he read the truth in her eyes, finding his intense gaze unsettling. 'I've had far too much to occupy my time.'

'Speaking of weddings—you know why I am here, don't you?'

'Of course. You have come for my answer to your proposal of marriage.'

Again that infuriating smile hovered on his lips. 'I thought you had given me your answer at Easterlea,' he said softly.

Lucinda tossed her head, angered by his conceit, and there was a stubborn set to her jaw as she met his gaze directly, but Laurence saw something move in the depths of her wonderful violet eyes. A tiny flame of triumph licked about his heart and he smiled.

'Then you thought wrong, sir. It should not be assumed that one kiss, given in the heat of the moment, is any kind of commitment. Your impudence astonishes me. There has not been sight nor sound of you for several weeks and you suddenly reappear out of the blue and come here, seeking an audience with my father, making a proposal of marriage to me—as though nothing unusual has occurred. Really, my lord, what am I to think?'

'You tell me, Miss Howard. What do you think?'

'Why—that you might be hard-pressed for my dowry,' she stated bluntly.

Her words made Laurence want to reach out and shake her for he knew that behind her bright expression and glib words the real passionate Lucinda he had glimpsed that night at Easterlea was still to be found. When he searched her face there was no longer any laughter in his eyes. He frowned and when he spoke it was on a more serious note.

'The estate does make claims on me that I cannot fail to take care of. That I cannot deny. And you may think what you will, but when I came to see your father and made my proposal it was not of your wealth that I was thinking.'

Lucinda flushed scarlet, remembering that her Aunt Celia had told her how deeply Lord Rainborough cared for her. Could this be true? The knowledge that it could be so acted on her like an intoxicating potion.

'And,' Laurence continued, holding her eyes in a penetrating gaze, 'I have no intention of leaping into an alliance with some other offering a golden dowry until I have your answer. So, come. What is it to be? Will you be my wife?'

Lucinda stared at him, swallowing hard, wanting so much to say yes, that nothing would make her happier—but still she held back, feeling a restraint in him. She had not imagined their meeting to be like this, with a distance between them. She had waited for him to come for her answer to his proposal with feverish anticipation. Nothing had prepared her for this polite, remote stranger who stood before her. If only he had taken her in his arms and murmured soft, tender words of love to give her confidence to overcome the difficulties she found in making her decision. But there was nothing. Perhaps marriage to him would bring her all these things, but for now she must content herself with things as they were.

The joy she had felt upon seeing him, which had temporarily obliterated all else, had explained her feelings towards him—there was no point in denying them any longer. But she could not commit herself to anything until certain matters had been explained.

'Forgive me,' she said, endeavouring to keep her tone light, 'but I feel that I cannot accept your proposal until certain matters have been cleared up.'

He looked surprised. 'Which are?'

'The—the woman I saw you with in York. The Spanish woman and the child. You must understand that, if I do agree to become your wife, it is only right that I know about her. Is—is she your mistress?'

At any other time Laurence would have thrown back his head and roared with laughter at such a ridiculous suggestion, but the moment was too serious to make light of.

He became thoughtful, his expression unreadable. 'You are right. You should know—and you must believe me when I say that I had every intention of telling you about them—and why I left Easterlea with such haste.' He continued to look at her hard, concern filling his eyes, as though willing her to understand what he was about to disclose. 'The child is my daughter. Maria—the woman she was with—is her nurse.'

Thrown completely off balance, Lucinda stared at him uncomprehendingly. 'Your—your daughter? But—but I don't understand. Why didn't you tell me? Shouldn't you have told me of her existence before you asked me to marry you?'

'Perhaps,' he said. 'But would it have made any difference if I had to your decision—as to whether or not you accepted my offer of marriage?'

Utterly confused, Lucinda frowned and turned from him. 'I—I don't think so,' she said hesitantly, 'but, nevertheless, you should have told me. Why all the secrecy? And where is her mother?'

His silence prompted her to turn and look at him.

'Her mother—my wife—is dead.' Laurence's eyes darkened with sadness and his voice was flat and heavy with emotion. 'She suffered a difficult birth and died soon after Christina, our daughter, was born.'

'I see,' whispered Lucinda, feeling a tightening around her heart. 'I am so sorry. Please— tell me what happened after that?'

'It is not a happy tale, but you have a right to

hear it. Because of my commitment to the army, I was unable to take care of her. In any case, it was better for all concerned that she remained in a stable environment—with her grandfather—Don Philippe de Silva.' He spoke the name with an underlying bitterness which did not escape Lucinda. 'When word reached me of Rupert's death and my inheritance—knowing I would have to return to England, I took Christina away from her grandfather.'

He moved away from Lucinda towards the window and stared out over the garden, seeming to forget for the moment that she was there. As he had been speaking, his voice had become quiet and there was a softness to his face she had not seen before. For the first time she saw a different side to him.

'Fortunately, Maria was as devoted to Christina as she had been to my wife, Isabella. I was grateful when she agreed to accompany us to England.'

'And Don Philippe, Christina's grandfather? He must surely miss her?'

Laurence's expression became grim, his eyes as hard as granite. 'Don Philippe is an extremely rich, formidable man and he has great power, owning vast estates north of Cadiz. He is lord of his domain and must be obeyed by all. Whoever disobeys him must be prepared to suffer the consequences. Many in Cadiz went in fear of him—many families he held in the palm of his hand. Isabella was his only child and Don Philippe worshipped her. When she died he was broken-hearted. After that he shifted all his affection to Christina—becoming quite obsessive about her. He did his best to prevent me taking her from him. It was an ugly scene—one I would not wish to repeat. But as her father I had right on my side—which is not a word Don Philippe is familiar with.'

Laurence turned and looked to where Lucinda had gone to sit on the settee, her hands folded on her lap as she listened to him.

'It is hard to tell you how different the Spanish are,' he continued. 'Although I expect you may have encountered some out in the Indies. There is a fierce, barbaric side to their nature—their Latin blood, I expect, which Don Philippe has inherited in full measure. He has sworn to get Christina back whatever it takes—and I do not underestimate his propensity to do so. I believe he is capable of resorting to any kind of treachery to accomplish this.' A murderous gleam entered his eyes. 'I am equally determined that he will not succeed.'

A thought suddenly occurred to Lucinda, causing a coldness to creep over her. 'Those men—the men we encountered at Easterlea—'

A savagery entered Laurence's voice, his words silencing her. 'Yes. They have been sent by Don Philippe. I am certain of it. Where they are now I know not—but it proves that I was right to fear for Christina's safety.'

'Where is she now? Why did you not bring her to Rainborough?'

'On my return to England, not knowing what awaited me at Rainborough, my main concern was to ensure Christina's safety. I left her with Maria in York, where they are staying with trusted friends of mine for the time being.'

A silence fell between them, allowing Lucinda to take stock of what he had told her. It had all come as quite a shock. She was relieved to know the woman, Maria, was the child's nurse and not his mistress, but the fact that he'd been married and that his wife had died, cast a cloud over her. And then another thought occurred to her. Hadn't he intimated that he had another reason for asking her to be his wife other than her dowry, raising her hopes to believe it was because he cared for her— when all the time his motive for doing so might be because he wanted a mother for his child?

'From what I remember of your daughter, she is extremely pretty,' she murmured. 'Is—is she like her mother?'

'Yes. Isabella was a woman of exceptional beauty.'

'Since her loss, Christina must have been a

great comfort to you. Is she the reason for your absence these past weeks?'

'Yes. I received word at Easterlea that she had been taken ill—that the worst was feared. I thought of nothing else but getting to her as quickly as I could.'

Lucinda nodded slightly, understanding at last the reason for his hasty departure from Easterlea. 'I can understand that. She is well now, I take it?'

'Yes—she survived, thank God. She is quite well—but for a time...' He turned away suddenly, his voice thickening with emotion as he remembered how close she had come to death.

Lucinda would have liked to offer comfort— but he was remote from her. Tenderness had entered his voice when he spoke of his daughter. He spoke lightly but she sensed his pain, the agony behind his words of what he must have endured—fearful lest his daughter should die. Lucinda was consumed with shame when she remembered how she had selfishly thought of little else but her own unhappy predicament during his absence.

'You must tell your cousin, Lady Lampton, what you have just told me. From the conversation I had with her before I left Easterlea I gather she is quite concerned about you especially when you left so hastily without an explanation.'

Laurence laughed softly, the faintly derisory gleam that she was beginning to know so well back in his eyes. 'I'm sure she is. It wouldn't be Beatrice if she wasn't concerned. Ever since my father died she always did worry about me — rather like a big sister.'

'Why did you not tell anyone about Christina? Why keep her existence a secret?'

'While ever there is a threat to her safety I could not take the risk of exposing her. The fewer people who know of her existence, the less chance any would-be abductors, sent by her grandfather to England, would have of finding her.'

'Have you told my father any of this?'

'Yes. He has known from the outset. It was only right that he should if I was to become Henrietta's husband. Your aunt knows, also. Now, tell me?' he asked quietly, a softness entering his eyes. 'Does what I have told you make a difference to your answer as to whether or not you will become my wife?'

Lucinda rose from the settee and moved a little closer to where he stood, forcing herself to think calmly. Gazing at his face, she knew the answer. She'd known it all along. She loved him. When she had begun to love him she did not know. It was something that had crept up on her slowly, but she had never been more certain of anything in her life before.

Yes, she loved this infuriating, unpredictable, insufferable man and there was not a thing she could do about it. The feeling was so deep, so strong, that on a wild impulse she came close to confessing the truth, but on seeing an image of his child and thinking of his dead wife, whom he must have loved—might still love—she recollected herself.

What difference did it make what his motives were for asking her to be his wife—her dowry or to be a mother to his child? The main thing was that he had and more than anything she wanted the love of this man. Before he had told her any of this she had felt the promise of love between them, that some strange chemistry had drawn them together. Of this she was not mistaken. Her Aunt Celia had been right when she had told her to have the courage to take things as they were in the hope that one day he would come to love her too.

She summoned up the courage to smile. 'I cannot pretend that what you have told me has not come as something of a surprise—but the knowledge that you have a child will not make any difference to my decision as to whether or not I accept your proposal of marriage.'

'Then why do you frown? And why the troubled, unsure look in your eyes?'

'Is there? I didn't know. Perhaps because I have difficulty sorting out my thoughts just now.

I am confused by all you have told me, certainly.'

'That is to be expected.' His voice was gentle. He cupped her face in his hand and stared down at her with an extraordinary tenderness. 'I think you are finding it difficult to understand the reason why I have asked you to be my wife. Is that it?'

His face was quite close to hers and Lucinda gazed up at him. Seeing in her eyes that this was so he sighed, smiling a little ruefully.

'You may rest assured it has nothing to do with your dowry. Let us be clear on that, shall we? I find the idea of marrying someone for their inheritance as loathsome as you do. Nor have I asked you to be my wife because I feel my daughter is in need of a mother. Christina has ample love and devotion bestowed upon her by myself and her nurse never to want for more.'

'So—neither one's your motive,' Lucinda said softly, waves of great happiness sweeping over her as she anticipated his declaration of love.

'No. You are a lovely, desirable woman, Lucinda,' he said, addressing her by her Christian name for the first time. 'Any man would be proud to have you for his wife. There is a fascinating, unique quality about you that I find appealing—so—who else would I ask to be my wife but the one who inspires me with emotions I have never felt before? Besides,' he smiled, 'I believe you were destined to be a countess whatever your feelings happen to be regarding the subject. So what do you say?'

Lucinda smiled, hiding the disappointment she felt by his omission of the word love, and yet a sense of hope raced through her. They would come to know each other fully. The promise was there in his eyes and the hope that he loved her grew stronger.

'Of course I cannot pretend that life will be easy at Rainborough,' he continued, 'but in time things will improve. Also, I have to tell you that there will be occasions when I must be in London so I intend reopening the house my uncle bought in Kensington. Does that appeal to you?'

'That isn't important. I am of the same mind as Lord Lampton and cannot understand why everyone should want to be in London all the time—surrounded as we are by the delights and pleasures of the countryside.'

'Nevertheless, there will be times when you will hanker for the gay life of the London social scene—for the theatre and the balls where you can enjoy yourself. It will be an exciting diversion from the quietude of Rainborough where there are few distractions. Arrangements must also be made for you to be presented at court.'

Lucinda looked at him with amused amazement, her lips quirking at the corners as she tried to suppress a smile. 'I am well able to enjoy myself perfectly well here in the country—although I would deem it a great honour to be presented at court, I do admit. But you are presumptuous, my lord. As yet I have not said I will marry you.'

'No. But I hope you will,' he said quietly.

'Then you will have to be patient for I feel that I would like to get to know Christina a little better before I commit myself.'

Laurence nodded. 'That is understandable. I am to return to York to bring her to Rainborough before the roads become too bad for me to travel. I also fear that by rushing to be by her side when she was taken ill I may have exposed her to danger—that the men we saw at Easterlea—who had also been sighted in Rainborough before that—may have followed me there in the hope that I would lead them to Christina.'

'Why did you not bring her with you when you returned to Rainborough a week ago?'

'She was still recovering from her illness and was too weak to travel when I left, otherwise I would have done so. Perhaps you would care to accompany me when I return? If leaving your father concerns you, then if you do decide to come with me we should not be absent for more than two or three days at the most.'

'Why—Lord Rainborough, I—'

He held up his hand, reaching out and placing his fingers gently on her lips, silencing her. 'No more Lord Rainborough, Lucinda. I do find it rather tedious. My name is Laurence. It is agreed?'

She nodded. 'Very well—Laurence. I would very much like to go with you. When do you intend leaving?'

'The day after tomorrow. Does that suit you?'

'Perfectly,' she replied. 'I shall look forward to it.'

Laurence and Lucinda travelled to York with Nancy accompanying Lucinda. With the onset of winter the weather was cold but dry and fortunately the roads were still passable. Although Lucinda hadn't given Laurence her answer as to whether or not she would become his wife, she discovered a new kind of happiness which was a revelation to her. The sensation of being so close to him she found exciting and exhilarating, although she still didn't know how he felt towards her. Often she would sense him watching her and when she turned her head and met his gaze there was a warmth and an odd gleam in their dark depths which would disappear instantly, leaving her wondering as to what was going on behind his bland façade.

A new relationship had developed between

them. He was kindness itself, showing her the utmost courtesy—in fact it was as if all thoughts of that night at Easterlea had never happened. But often she found herself wishing to see a spark of the insufferable Lord Rainborough of old.

It was dark when the coach trundled through the archway and into the yard at Metcalfe Hall, where they were met by Anthony and his wife Margaret. Introductions were made quickly as they were ushered into the warmth of the house, passing out of a long panelled hall and into a large cosy room with a fireplace in which a welcoming fire glowed. Once again Lucinda came face to face with Maria, the dark-haired Spanish woman she had met in York, and the child, Laurence's daughter, who was leaping up and down with excitement.

'Christina should be in bed,' explained Maria in her heavily accented Spanish voice, 'but knowing her father was to come, she has been excited all day.'

Whatever notions of constraint and aloofness Lucinda might have had where Laurence was concerned, they were dispelled when she watched as he scooped his daughter up into his arms. His deep, protective love of the child was evident, which brought a lump of emotion to her throat and also a secret envy of the little girl, wishing it was upon her he was lavishing all this love and affection.

Christina was so like her father that it was a wonder Lucinda hadn't seen it from the outset. Clearly she had inherited the same dark colouring and gleaming black hair of her mother, but the brown eyes, with their steady gaze, and the square set of her jaw, bore the same marks of stubborn determination as her father.

When Laurence brought her over to meet Lucinda, who was hovering, vaguely uneasy, in the doorway, it was not as difficult as she had imagined making friends with Christina. She was an adorable, gregarious child who made friends easily.

'This is Miss Howard, Christina,' explained Laurence softly. 'She is a very good friend of mine and would very much like to be your friend, too. Come—say hello to her. I have told her all about my little Christina and she has been looking forward to meeting her.'

Christina needed no further prompting from her doting father, for she gave Lucinda a dazzling smile which melted Lucinda's heart, dispelling any misgivings she might have had about meeting her. When Christina reached out from her father's arms and placed her own about her neck, drawing her close and placing a gentle kiss on her cheek, Lucinda's eyes filled with tears. Meeting Laurence's eyes, who was smiling with concern and understanding, for he knew how much this moment had worried her, she lowered her gaze quickly, ashamed of herself for showing her emotions.

When Laurence had handed his daughter to Maria, promising to come and see her the moment she was in bed, he turned to Lucinda.

'She is a truly delightful child,' murmured Lucinda.

'Yes. I am so lucky to have her. I'm sure the two of you will become friends—and I hope, in time, you will grow to love her as much as I.'

Gazing up at him, Lucinda's eyes were captured and held by his and she was stirred by the depth of warmth and sincerity in his voice. She felt that above all else it was important to him that she came to love his daughter—that it was what he had intended all along. She realised that if she married Laurence then she would be needed—not only by her husband but also by his daughter, and this thought warmed and excited her.

At that moment Margaret came to stand beside them.

'A room has been made ready for you, Lucinda. There is a room next to it for Nancy, your maid. Come—I'll show you the way myself and after you have refreshed yourself we shall eat. I'm sure you must be quite ravenous.'

Slightly perplexed, Lucinda looked at her.

'That is thoughtful of you, Margaret. But, a room made ready for me, you say? How could you possibly know I was coming?'

Realising she had made a *faux pas* Margaret looked with helpless appeal from Lucinda to Laurence, who stepped quickly forward to redeem the situation.

'I took the liberty of telling Margaret and her husband that you might accompany me when I returned for Christina.'

'Oh! You're very sure of yourself,' she exclaimed.

His dark eyes danced with some of the old mischief and he grinned. 'Where you are concerned, my dear Lucinda, I have to be.'

Margaret took her up to her room, which was low ceilinged with pale green curtains at the window and matching ones on the canopied bed and with warming pans already between the sheets. It was a charming, well-furnished, restful room overlooking the street. A fire burning in the hearth generated a warmth Lucinda found welcoming. She moved to look out of the window, the faint moonlight outlining the rooftops and steeples and towers of the many churches of York.

'I'm so happy that you agreed to accompany Laurence to York, Lucinda,' said Margaret coming to stand beside her. 'He told us so much about you when he came to see Christina.'

Lucinda turned and looked at her, feeling somewhat surprised and pleased to discover he had not forgotten about her altogether when he had left Easterlea.

'He did?'

'Yes,' she smiled. 'He also told us that you have lived for most of your life on Barbados— that you did not come to England until about a year ago. You will find it all so much different, I expect?'

'Yes. It's certainly colder—but I am becoming accustomed to it.'

'It's good, don't you think,' said Margaret changing the subject, 'that Laurence is taking Christina back to Rainborough? There he will be able to devote more time to her.'

'Yes, although the threat from Don Philippe—Christina's grandfather—worries him considerably. With the estate to run he'll find it extremely difficult keeping his eye on her all the time.'

'That I know, but for the time being he will have to put more work and the management of estate affairs into the hands of his bailiffs. Of course he has William—his valet at Rainborough—who was with him throughout his years with the army. He's a worthy, trusty man, who takes his duties seriously. I'm sure he can be relied upon to watch over Christina when Laurence is absent—especially with Maria at Rainborough.'

She smiled when Lucinda glanced at her questioningly. 'I got a distinct impression when they first came to York—when Laurence left William here until Christina and Maria were settled with us—that they are extremely fond of each other. But tell me, Lucinda, what do you think of Christina? She's an adorable child, don't you think? Anthony and I will miss her terribly when she's no longer here with us.'

'Wh-what do you know of her mother?' asked Lucinda hesitantly. 'Does Laurence ever speak of her?'

Margaret shook her head. 'No. All we know is that she died almost as soon as Christina was born. It's sad when you think she never knew her mother. I suppose Maria is the closest she has to one.' She frowned suddenly, moving towards the bed and absently smoothing the covers. 'I have to say that I'm quite concerned about Maria. She's been edgy and quiet of late—not her usual self. Of course she wore herself out looking after Christina during her illness, refusing to leave her bedside for a moment in case anything should happen to her. I don't suppose it's good for her being cooped up here all the time. She's become so restless.'

'Does she not go out of the house?'

'No—at least, not often. Laurence made it

absolutely clear that Christina must remain in doors at all times—which is strictly adhered to. But Maria—just once or twice this past week—has slipped out of the house to take the air.'

'Maybe she will cease to be so restless when she goes to Rainborough—and perhaps I will be able to help.'

Margaret looked at her sharply, a gleam of hope entering her eyes. 'Forgive me if I am speaking out of place, Lucinda. I—I know it's none of my business—but—do you intend marrying Laurence?'

Lucinda met her gaze directly. 'I don't mind you asking, Margaret. He has asked me to be his wife but I have not, as yet, given him my answer.'

'I see. I—I hope you will say yes. He is a splendid man—a very special person, and he speaks very highly of you. And I can see you are head over heels in love with him. Is that not so?'

Lucinda sighed deeply, aware that Margaret and her husband had known Laurence for many years, that they were close friends. Since entering the house, she'd had the feeling that Margaret had been assessing her as to her suitability of becoming Laurence's wife, and she assumed, by the pleased look on her face, that she approved.

'You are extremely perceptive, Margaret—

and you are right,' she acknowledged honestly. 'I do love him a great deal.'

'Then why do you not tell him?'

'I cannot. Not yet. You see—I've only just become aware of it myself—and also that Christina is his daughter—that he has a daughter, in fact. I've had no experience with children and wish to get to know her a little before I commit myself.'

'I can understand that,' said Margaret softly, 'but it shouldn't be too difficult. Christina is a very loving, tactile child. You'll soon get to know her—if—as we all hope, you decide to marry Laurence, of course.'

'But of course,' replied Lucinda, and the two laughed, already with that close camaraderie of friendship.

Lucinda was wonderfully happy during the following day which was spent with Laurence and Christina. Laurence was indefatigable in his attempts to please her and Lucinda gave herself up to the sheer enjoyment of letting him. She learned a great deal, not only about his daughter but also about him—how knowledgable he was about music and art, that he nurtured a long-held love of good horseflesh and country pursuits and how, in the future, when he had put Rainborough back on its feet, he intended filling the stables at Rainborough Castle with fine bloodstock. He loved to talk at length about his time spent in the army, serving under the great Duke of Marlborough at Blenheim and later in Spain, although he took care to avoid any mention of his dead wife, Isabella, showing a certain caution in speaking at all of that personal side of his life.

They were to leave for Rainborough the following morning and although Lucinda had felt there had been a certain restraint in Laurence throughout the day, nevertheless, by the time she went to bed she was physically tired and extremely happy—a happiness which was brutally shattered when she awoke the following morning to find the whole household in turmoil.

Both Maria and Christina had disappeared from the house during the night.

# CHAPTER ELEVEN

IT WAS in the chill light of dawn when Laurence became aware of Christina's disappearance. Margaret's voice was frantic as she told him. At first he stared at her wordlessly, distinctly feeling his heart almost stop beating in his chest as he tried to comprehend her words, but then, understanding that she was telling him that his worst fears had been realised, that his daughter had been taken, his eyes sprang to life.

He flung himself towards the door, his formidable anger bursting from him and vibrating around the walls of the room, directed not at Margaret or Lucinda, who stood by in anxious silence, but at Don Philippe and the men he had sent to abduct his daughter and Maria's treacherous stupidity for allowing it to happen.

His face white with pain, Laurence left the house to go in search of his daughter, while the only thing Lucinda and Margaret could do was anxiously await his return. Having left early for his office of work in Petergate, close to the Minster, Anthony was unaware that anything was amiss. The nervous strain of Christina's disappearance was almost too much for

Margaret, for she should have known, from Maria's strange behaviour of the past week, that something was wrong, but she had trusted her implicitly with the care of Christina, as did everyone.

When Laurence finally returned to the house, his face was set and grim. Seeing his strained features, sensing his tortured frame of mind, his grief and fury which he kept in abeyance, Lucinda was aware that beneath his remarkable self-control, which his military training had taught him to employ, he was a man in the grip of a nightmare. All his years as a soldier, of experiencing the horrendous, bloody realities of warfare and witnessing the appalling sufferings of men, could not add up to what he was suffering now.

Lucinda met him in the hall as he entered, placing a trembling hand on his arm. 'Oh, Laurence, thank goodness you're back. Tell me — is there any news?'

'No. None. Have you checked to see if any of their clothes are missing?'

'Yes. Margaret is certain that some are gone.'

'Then this in itself is suspicious, for it can only mean that Maria was in league with the abductors — that she must have had contact with them at some time.'

'Margaret did say that she left the house twice in the past week and that she has been quiet and withdrawn. But why would she do this?'

'Normally she wouldn't—but I strongly suspect that Don Philippe has threatened in some way her or her family, who live and work on his estate near Cadiz. I suspect that she agreed to their demands to give them Christina out of fear of what Don Philippe will do should she not comply. I should have realised this would happen when I agreed for her to come to England as Christina's nurse, that he would use her as a pawn in his game to get her back.'

'Dear Lord,' whispered Lucinda, 'the man must be a monster. Have you been to the Black Swan in Coney Street to enquire as to whether or not they boarded the London coach?'

He nodded. 'It was the first place I went to. There was no one fitting their description on board. The fact that they were not on the London coach and that none of the wardens or constables have seen them leave by any of the gates—for at the time they left the city would have been quiet, with hardly anyone about— leaves me with a flicker of hope that they are still within the city itself—in hiding until the hue and cry dies down before leaving. Unless, of course, they were well organised and a conveyance was waiting, in which case they will have made good their escape and could be well away from the city by this time—on their way to one of the country's ports—perhaps Bristol in the West Country. There they will find a ship bound for Spain.'

'Then maybe you should dispatch someone to check the roads, just in case,' suggested Lucinda.

'I have already done so. The wardens and parish constables are also searching and there is strict watch being kept on all the gates out of York. Anyone matching Maria and Christina's descriptions are to be apprehended—as are the two Spaniards.' He sighed deeply, running his fingers impatiently through his hair which had come loose from its cue, the rain which had started to fall from a leaden sky having caused it to curl in a thick wet mass. 'I must go. I only returned to the house to see if—by some chance—she had returned.'

'But you cannot go on aimlessly searching.'

A look of desperation entered his eyes. 'I have to, Lucinda. What else can I do?'

'But where? Where will you look?'

A thunderous frown drew his black eyebrows together in a single line as he contemplated his daughter's plight, and when he thought of her in the hands of Don Philippe's henchmen a red haze began to rise in front of his eyes.

'I will turn York inside out if need be to find her.' Looking down intently into Lucinda's upturned face, its whiteness emphasised by the dark green colour of her dress, he suddenly reached out and took her in his arms, burying his lips in her hair as he held her tightly in his arms, the fear that he might be too late, that despite all his methods to protect his daughter Don Phllippe might succeed in getting back his granddaughter, weighing him down so that he could hardly stand it. 'I must find her, Lucinda. I must.'

Closing her eyes, Lucinda melted against him, wishing with all her heart that he had taken her into his embrace under different circumstances. She wrapped her arms around him, deeply aware of his aching desolation and wishing she could find words to comfort him. But there were none. Whatever words she offered would be sadly inadequate.

'You will, Laurence,' she said softly. 'You will find her—and she is with Maria. Whatever part she played in her abduction, she loves her as she would her own child. She will see to it that she comes to no harm.'

Raising his head and gazing down into her enormous eyes, awash with unshed tears of sympathy, they each uttered a silent passionate prayer to God that she was right.

Their inner unease communicated itself to each other as the time Lucinda and Margaret waited for Laurence to return to the house dragged slowly by, the tension in the air intensified by the wind which was beginning to rise, and the rain steadily pattering against the window panes. Suddenly Margaret rose from the chair in which she was seated, her hand going to her mouth in alarm as a thought suddenly occurred to her.

'Oh, my goodness—Anthony—he—he doesn't know what's happened. He left so early for his office of work that he is totally unaware that Christina is missing. I must send someone to tell him.'

Lucinda stood up quickly. 'No—wait, Margaret. I know where Anthony's offices are. I'll go and tell him.'

'You?'

'Yes. I'll be all right. I'll take Nancy with me.' Seeing Margaret's frown she sighed. 'I must do something,' she explained, 'or else I'll go mad if I have to sit and wait much longer.'

And so, with Nancy to accompany her, Lucinda set off down Micklegate, wrapped in a warm cloak with her hood pulled well over her head to shield her from the gently falling rain, having to tread carefully for the cobbles had become wet and slippery under foot. Hurriedly they made their way towards Ouse Bridge, crossing it and moving on up Ouse Gate. Here they had to pause and wait, unable to move on, for a Civic procession was in progress—one of various official entertainments the citizens were often presented with. They stood at the side of the street, watching as it passed by. At any other time Lucinda would have been fascinated to watch this diversion, more than likely the welcoming of an important visitor to York, which entertained and enlivened the streets. Lucinda sighed, impatient for it to pass on so that she could cross the street.

She let her eyes wander over the slow-moving procession, seeing the Mayor and Aldermen in their distinctive scarlet gowns, the Sheriffs in crimson and the wealthier citizens parading in their finest apparel. A number of Waits with silver chains and red livery coats provided ceremonial music, their long woodwind instruments making a raucous sound in the narrow streets.

The people began to disperse as the procession passed on. As Lucinda was about to move away, a movement in the crowd across the street caught her eye. She saw a man shoving his way through—not that there was anything unusual in this, but there was something about this man that caught and held all her attention, for the black greasy hair, swarthy skin and the narrow-beaked nose she recognised immediately as belonging to one of the Spanish men she had seen at Easterlea—one of the men they were certain was responsible for Christina's disappearance.

Unable to believe her eyes, believing that providence had surely stepped in, Lucinda stood as if rooted to the spot, causing Nancy, who was impatient to move on and follow the procession along Pavement, to look at her curiously. She was quite unprepared when Lucinda, seeing the man slip up a side alley, grasped her hand and began pulling her in the opposite direction from the one in which they were supposed to be heading.

'Miss Lucinda,' she protested. 'Where are we going? Petergate's the other way.'

'I know it is, Nancy, but I'm sure I've just seen one of the men we believe is responsible for abducting Christina go up that alleyway. We must follow him. He might lead us to where they are hiding her. Oh—please, come along,' she pleaded, exasperated when Nancy began to pull back, her eyes wide and her mouth agape in disbelief.

'Lord, Miss Lucinda—how can you be sure it's the same man?'

'Because I've seen him before. I'm certain it was him. Now hurry. If we stand here arguing, we'll lose him altogether.'

Under the determined pressure in her mistress's eyes and sensing the urgency in her tone, knowing better than to utter any further objections, Nancy did as she was told. Together they hurried across the street and entered the alleyway up which the man had just disappeared.

One thought and one thought only drove Lucinda on—to keep the man in her sights at all times, not to lose him at any cost. She paid no heed to the dark, twisting narrow alleyways they ran along, careful to keep far enough behind so as not to arouse his suspicion that he was being followed.

He hurried along ahead of them, a shabby black coat flapping about his legs. They crossed a bridge spanning the River Foss, entering the gruesome, twilight world of Walmgate, a part of York Lucinda had never imagined existed. It was as if she had left heaven and descended into hell.

Few places could be worse than this, where ugliness and poverty went hand in hand. Centuries-old, tightly packed, ramshackle overhanging buildings rose on either side, with crumbling gables and plasterwork, dingy and foul, housing the dregs of humanity—the poor, the destitute—offering a refuge for villains and ruffians alike, away from the eyes of the law.

Ill-humoured voices and cursing could be heard from within the dwellings and people in rags, with lustreless eyes in deep-set sockets, lounged in doorways, giving them no more than a passive glance as they passed by. Rain dripped onto them from jettied roofs and mud oozed up from between the cobbles. They kept their cloaks wrapped tight about them in an attempt to stop them becoming soiled on the middens, but the streets were so narrow it was almost an impossible task.

The stench of Walmgate was all-pervading, the reek of putrefaction everywhere. Lucinda had never seen anything like this before. How could people live in this place? Both she and Nancy had to cover their noses against the ageless odour from mounds of rotting filth and garbage piled up outside doors, leaving nothing to the imagination of their contents. During warmer, summer months, when the air would be thick with the buzz of blue bottles, it would be a haven for disease.

Pigs squealed and cattle lowed miserably in the back yards of slaughter houses, awaiting their fate, at which time their blood would flow out into the congested gutters in the middle of the streets, where grey-skinned, barefoot children, with matted hair and huge, deep, ringed eyes in dirt-grimed faces, played, seemingly indifferent to it all because they knew nothing else, sadly unaware there was another world outside Walmgate. If it were not for the man they were following and the importance of her quest, Lucinda would have turned and run out of this nightmare world which God had passed by.

The man entered a cobbled yard with heaps of straw piled high. Pausing and standing out of his view, Lucinda and Nancy watched him climb a high flight of rickety wooden stairs to an upper storey of a tall building and disappear through a door. With bated breath they waited, unsure what to do next as they watched the closed door, their eyes scanning the one small grimy window next to it. A movement from within caught Lucinda's sharp eyes and suddenly she felt a surge of hope, for she was sure it was a child's face she saw looking out. Excitedly she turned to Nancy.

'Do you see, Nancy? There's Christina. I'm sure of it.'

Nancy shook her head dumbly, her one thought to be gone from this foul place. 'I don't know, Miss Lucinda. It's hard to tell who it is from down here.'

'I'm sure it's her,' she said, breathing excitedly. 'I want you to hurry back to Metcalfe Hall, Nancy. I'll stay here and wait.'

At the full implication of her words Nancy gasped. 'Oh, Miss Lucinda—you don't mean to go into that place?'

'Not unless I have to—which I will do if necessary. Now, go and get Lord Rainborough—and don't dawdle. Tell him he must come quickly.' When she saw the terror staring out of Nancy's eyes, for she was fearful of going back through those streets alone, in irritation Lucinda gave her a push. 'Nothing's going to happen to you if you hurry. Go along, Nancy—and don't you dare get lost—do you hear? Remember that in all probability Christina is in that room. Her safety depends on how soon you can come back with Lord Rainborough. Do you understand?'

Dumbly she swallowed hard and nodded and reluctantly, knowing better than to argue and, holding her skirts tightly about her, Nancy started off down the warren of alleyways in the direction they had come.

Alone, Lucinda stood in the shadows watching the building, people about her scarcely giving her a second glance. After about half an hour the door at the top of the wooden staircase opened and two men emerged, causing Lucinda's heart to soar with a sense of triumph, for one was the man she had followed and the other was the taller, stockier man she had seen with him at Easterlea.

Together they descended the stairs to the yard, deep in conversation as they came towards Lucinda, who stepped behind the stone pillar of the gateway out of sight. They passed close to where she stood and she heard their voices, unable to understand any of what they said for they spoke in their native Spanish.

She watched as they disappeared down the street before turning her attention back to the room at the top of the stairs, where she suspected Maria and Christina would be alone. Dare she risk going up there? Without further hesitation, knowing there was no time to lose, sheer determination galvanised her into action and she ran across the yard and gingerly mounted the stairs, feeling they were none too safe as they seemed to sway the higher she got.

The door gave way beneath her fingers as she pushed it and stepped inside an upper room of a draughty, creaking house, straining her eyes in the gloom. It was cold and had a sour, stale smell, the walls peeling with damp plasterwork and filthy curtains hanging at the tiny unwashed window, letting little light into the room.

As her eyes became accustomed to the dark, she stepped round a pail of slops close to the door, seeing a woman sitting on a straw pallet next to the wall, a small child with frightened eyes held close to her breast. Lucinda breathed a sigh of relief. It was Christina. There was no welcome in Maria's eyes whose arms tightened around her charge, perhaps fearing Lucinda would attempt to snatch her from her.

'What are you doing here?' she cried, rising from the pallet. 'Don't you know it ees dangerous for you? If Alonso and Miguel return and find you here there ees no telling what they will do. Miguel—he ees my brother and ees not a violent man but Alonso can do bad things when he ees angry. You must go back.'

'No, Maria,' said Lucinda, crossing over to her. 'Not without Christina. However, thank God you are both safe. Whatever your reasons for taking Christina from her father, you must come back. Please—I implore you. Think of the grief your actions have caused him.'

'No. I cannot return. I think only of the pain and grief my own family will suffer if I do not do this.'

'Why? Has Don Philippe threatened them, Maria?' asked Lucinda gently, trying to maintain an air of calm while having to resist the urge to grab Christina from her and take her back to her father.

'Don Philippe ees a man to be feared. He has promised to throw my family—my mother and father and brothers and sisters, out of their home—run them out of Cadiz if I do not comply with his orders and return Christina to him. Out of the love and duty I feel for them I cannot let him do this.' Tears suddenly filled Maria's dark eyes as she tried to make Lucinda understand the sheer hopelessness of her situation, that she had no choice but to obey Don Philippe.

'You cannot know what this will mean to them. They are poor people, Miss Howard, and rely on Don Philippe for everything—for the food they eat, their work, their very existence. You do not know what he ees like—how cruel he can be. If my brother returns without Christina he will be made to suffer terribly. He will be made to suffer the penalty Don Philippe will inflict upon him for my disobedience. Don't you see? I have no choice. We have to go back—to do this thing.'

Lucinda stared at her, beginning to understand the enormity of the problem Don Philippe de Silva had placed upon this woman and her heart went out to her. But she must think of Christina. She was foremost on her list of priorities. She could not let Maria's sad plight detract her from getting the child out of that room and back to her father before Alonso and Miguel returned.

'If I could do anything at all to help you, Maria, believe me I would. But at this moment my main concern is Christina. You must know that what you are doing is wrong. She belongs with her father—with Lord Rainborough—not Don Philippe.'

The mention of her father's name made Christina begin to whimper softly and she rubbed her eyes from which tears were beginning to fall. Clearly she was distressed by all that had happened. Lucinda looked on in alarm as Maria tried to comfort her, but she would not be comforted and began to cry louder.

'You must see it is useless,' persisted Lucinda. 'None of you can escape. Lord Rainborough has every thoroughfare out of York watched.'

'Alonso will find a way. He has gone to arrange for a conveyance to take us out of here.'

At that moment Lucinda heard footsteps in the cobbled yard below. Her heart lurched and she felt sick with terror, fearing the Spaniards, Alonso and Miguel, had returned, and she shuddered at what they would do to her when they found their hiding place had been discovered.

Her thoughts turned in desperation to Nancy, and she prayed she'd managed to reach Metcalfe Hall and Laurence. She became frozen to the spot as she heard the thud of boots on the wooden boards of the stairs outside, edging backwards as they came ever closer, uttering a cry of alarm when the burly figure of Miguel—the one she thought must be Maria's brother because of facial similarities—stood in the doorway.

Uttering some sort of curse in Spanish upon seeing her, the man quickly strode inside, followed by Alonso, the man Lucinda had followed. Despite Lucinda's determination that she would not succumb to despair, she felt her spirits sinking when she looked into the cold, cruel eyes of the Spaniard, knowing she could expect no mercy from him. With hindsight, how she wished she'd resisted the impulse to come rushing up to this room. Why hadn't she remained where she was and waited for Laurence to arrive?

His thin face expressionless, Alonso came further into the room and, without meaning to do so, Lucinda felt herself shrink as he approached, watching her with his cruel gaze. Suddenly he smiled thinly, which Lucinda thought was more like the grimace of an animal.

'So, *señorita*, you have found our hiding place,' he said in almost perfect English, with just a hint of Spanish. 'How clever of you. How did you manage to do that?'

Lucinda's throat went dry as she struggled to keep her voice on a level, determined not to let her fear get the best of her. 'I saw you in the town and recognised you. I followed you here.'

'Ah—so—you have a good memory, *señorita*. I congratulate you. I must have made a strong impression on you that day you saw Miguel and me at that place by the sea. Tell me? What did you hope to achieve by coming here? Did you hope to persuade Maria to listen to you? To return the child to her father? Is that it?

Because if so, then you are wasting your time. Maria has made up her mind to go back to Spain.'

'Christina belongs here, in England, with her father,' replied Lucinda stiffly.

Alonso laughed, a thin, discordant sound which made Lucinda's blood run cold.

'Don Philippe does not think so. He thinks it best that she is brought up in Spain, in his home where her mother grew up, also.'

'Tell me?' Lucinda ventured bravely. 'Are you afraid of Don Philippe? Does he have a hold over you, too, in order to ensure that you do his bidding?'

Her words caused anger to flare in the Spaniard. His eyes became drawn together like slits, their sooty depths glowing like coals. Alonso had suffered all his life from a sense of frustration born out of poverty. Don Philippe de Silva had offered him a great deal if he could successfully locate his granddaughter in England and take her back to him in Spain.

Seeing a chance of becoming rich beyond his wildest dreams, he had sworn that if anyone should dare to cross or defy him they would soon learn that he possessed a cruel ruthlessness which stopped at nothing. Miss Lucinda Howard was just an interfering chit of an English girl. If necessary he would kill her.

'No one has a hold over Alonso Gonzalez.

No one,' he hissed fiercely. 'You are very bold, *señorita*. Too bold for your own good. But your request to Maria that she returns the child to her father comes a little late. I told you. She has no intention of giving her up.'

'Then you are out of your mind if you think you will succeed in getting her out of the country. Have you not thought what the consequence of your actions will be when you are caught?'

'If we are caught,' he growled, thrusting his face closer to hers, 'which will not happen. We will be gone from here quite soon, and should you have any notions about raising the alarm then you can forget them. You should not have come here alone, *señorita*, for Walmgate is a notorious haven for criminals of every sort. Looking as you do there will be those who will remember seeing you. Many people who enter are never heard of again so no one will think it strange if you disappear. No one is going to find you for quite some time—if ever. The waters of your River Ouse are deep, the currents strong and fast. Your body will remain submerged for long enough and will be washed up far away from York.'

The overriding menacing threat of his last words smote terror in Lucinda and she froze. Her heart appeared to stop and she felt an icy shiver course over her skin, feeling the walls of the room beginning to close in on her, for she was in no doubt that his threat was serious. That he meant to kill her.

'So—you would kill me!'

'Let me say that we did not come all this way to have our plans foiled by anyone. I would not wish to kill a woman, but by coming here you have got in our way, *señorita*. I have no choice.'

Uttering a cry of alarm, Maria dropped Christina onto the pallet to go to Lucinda's aid but her brother, who had remained in the shadows, unable to converse with Lucinda for he knew little English, caught hold of her arm, indicating that she should not interfere.

Anger was beginning to overcome Lucinda's fear as she began to think about self-preservation. Sensitive to the tension, the threatening atmosphere that prevailed inside the room, Christina's whimpering once again changed to a loud wailing. Maria again scooped her up into her arms to quieten her, tightening her hold on her as her dark eyes apprehensively watched Alonso and Lucinda.

It was then that Lucinda became aware of the sound of voices in the yard below. Her eyes flew to the door for she was sure she could hear someone calling her name. Thinking that it had to be Laurence, that Nancy had managed to reach him, she made an involuntary move towards the door, opening her mouth to call out his name, but Alonso seized her by her slender wrist and clapped his claw-like hand over her mouth, silencing any sound she might have made.

A fearful struggle broke out between them, for at that moment Lucinda saw the flash of a blade appear in his hand as if from nowhere. Never before in her whole life had she been so stricken with terror as when she realised he wanted her life. Once again Maria tried to go to her aid, but her brother held her fast. No matter how hard she continued to struggle against him he did not release his hold, himself too fearful of Alonso to interfere.

Strength born out of fear and desperation came to Lucinda's aid and she fought like a tigress, twisting and clawing at his face. Alonso was surprised by the strength of her resistance but Lucinda was no match for him. She felt a searing hot pain in her side and knew she was wounded but she paid it no heed as she continued to fight.

Just when Alonso thought he had her within his grasp and was about to sink the blade into her soft flesh once more, she bit the hand that wielded knife so hard that he howled with pain and dropped it. Tasting his blood on her lips, Lucinda took advantage of the split second when he slackened his hold on her and darted towards the door, but he reached out and

yanked at her hair, pulling her back. A strangled cry of pain broke from her just as Alonso
gave her a brutal push and flung her to the
floor. She fell heavily, hitting her head hard
against the wall.

At that moment pandemonium broke out in
the room and the last things Lucinda was aware
of before darkness swirled over and engulfed
her, was a terrible pain in her side, Christina's
loud, frightened sobbing and Laurence's tall
shadow falling across the doorway.

# CHAPTER TWELVE

WHEN Nancy had arrived at Metcalfe Hall, Laurence had just returned in a desperate state. There seemed to be nothing he could do but just go on aimlessly searching. Nancy was breathless, having run all the way from Walmgate. It was several moments before she could speak coherently, but at last what had happened came out in a torrent of words, tumbling over each other. With Margaret standing anxiously beside him Laurence listened, hardly believing what she was saying, but if she was telling the truth, then this was the first dawning of hope since Christina's disappearance. But Lucinda? What of her? Why was she not here with Nancy?

Reaching out, he gripped her shoulders hard. 'Where is Lucinda? Why is she not here with you?'

'I—I left her there—in Walmgate.'

'What? You came back here without her?'

Laurence's shocked and incredulous voice brought tears to Nancy's eyes. 'I had to. I didn't want to but she made me,' she wailed, almost as afraid of the ice-cold, formidable look in

251

Lord Rainborough's eyes—the same that he would employ on a battlefield, she thought—as she had been of coming back alone through the alleyways of Walmgate.

'You say the man went up some stairs to the upper storey of a house in Walmgate?'

She nodded.

'And he was still up there when you left Lucinda?'

'Yes. Miss Lucinda said she would wait out-side—where I left her—that she wouldn't go in unless she had to.'

'Dear Lord,' said Laurence, his hands drop-ping down by his sides. 'I pray she hasn't done anything so foolish.'

He turned away to hide the anguish, the naked agony in his eyes. What was Lucinda thinking of? he asked himself, and he cursed her stubborn rebelliousness. Why hadn't she returned with Nancy to find him instead of trying to deal with this thing alone? Did she not realise the danger she had placed herself in? Wasn't it enough that he had come so close to losing Christina, without losing her, also?

He was under no illusions as to the kind of men Don Philippe would have sent to abduct his granddaughter. They would think nothing of killing Lucinda if she dared to get in their way. When he got her back he would never let her out of his sight again—ever, not as long as he lived, for he loved her, he worshipped her, and he would fight to keep her. He turned back to Nancy, again placing his hands on her shoulders and looking at her in earnest.

'You say she is certain it is the same man she saw at Easterlea?'

'Yes, sir. She—she was also positive it was Miss Christina she saw at the window looking out.'

'Then listen, Nancy,' Laurence said firmly, his grip on her shoulders tightening, forcing her to look at him. 'You must show me where she is. Can you remember?'

She nodded, alarm filling her eyes at the horrifying prospect of having to return to that dreadful place. 'Oh, my lord—don't make me go back there. I can't.'

'You have to. I am familiar as to what Walmgate is like—nothing but a rabbit warren of festering alleyways. While you're trying to tell me where the house is we could be half way there. Lucinda's life and my daughter's may depend on you, Nancy. You do understand that, don't you?'

'Yes,' she whispered.

'Good—then come along.' He turned to Margaret. 'I left two constables out in the street, Margaret. I'll take them with me. It is imperative that we get to Lucinda as quickly as possible so we'll have to go on foot. With all the congestion on the streets at this time a carriage would be too slow. Not knowing what I shall find when I get to this house in Walmgate, order the carriage to follow on behind, will you? Have it wait at the bridge over the Foss.'

Before Margaret could wish him well, to tell him to go with care, he was gone, dragging a reluctant Nancy behind him.

With Nancy to show him the way, for he would never have found it alone, and the two constables doing their best to keep up with him, Laurence finally stood in the yard in Walmgate where Nancy said she had left Lucinda. Now she was nowhere to be seen. In desperation, fearful for her safety, he called her name, looking around him, his eyes coming to rest on the wooden staircase running up the side of a building. There was an open doorway at the top.

Suddenly a cold chill travelled down his spine for somewhere, up there in that room, a woman screamed. Lucinda! He plunged towards the stairs and climbed up, maddened almost beyond reason, his heart hammering violently in his rush to reach the source of that scream. He paused in the doorway, just in time to see the Spaniard knock Lucinda to the floor and hear the sickening thud as her head hit the wall. She lay perfectly still.

Laurence's eyes swept the room, taking in the squalor. His heart soared with relief on seeing his daughter huddled on the dirty pallet sobbing miserably, clearly distressed but seemingly unhurt, and the other Spaniard holding Maria to prevent her from going to Lucinda's assistance. Seeing Lucinda lying senseless on the floor, hurt by the hands of this Spaniard sent by Don Philippe, he was filled with a blazing fury. His eyes were deadly when they came to rest on the Spaniard wielding the knife, having retrieved it from the floor where it had fallen in his struggle with Lucinda.

Alonso was slashing the air in an arc with the knife to keep Laurence at bay, his breathing guttural, his lips drawn back over his clenched teeth in a snarl as he waited for him to attack. Still holding Maria, who was watching the scene in a stunned silence, Miguel backed towards the wall, reluctant to partake in the violence which had erupted within the room.

Suddenly Alonso lunged towards Laurence with the knife, but his slight build was no match for his opponent's sheer physical strength, and he was unprepared when Laurence sprang towards him, grasping the hand which held the knife, causing Alonso to pitch over backwards. Laurence stamped on his wrist with such pressure that the hand opened and the knife became loose. He kicked it to the other side of the room. Alonso leaped to his feet, panting, looking for a way of escape and moving towards the open doorway, but Laurence was too quick for him and Alonso yelped as his hand shot out and fastened on his throat, jerking him up and slamming him against the door post.

Alonso's eyes rolled upwards, and lines of sweat were running down his cheeks and neck as he clawed at Laurence's hand squeezing his throat. Thrashing his legs, he knocked over the slop bucket and, grunting painfully, looked into Laurence's eyes. What he saw there made him realise that this man would show him no mercy, for they shone with a pitiless, deadly cold rage.

Suddenly Laurence released him. Slipping on the slops which had spilled over the floor, gagging, Alonso reeled backwards out of the doorway, hearing the splintering of wood as the loose balustrade gave way beneath the impact of his body falling against it. At first, surprise registered in his eyes, but then, with a strangled cry and frantically clutching at the empty air, he tumbled down into the yard below—where the constables and Nancy looked on in stupefaction—missing the foul heap of rotting garbage which would have broken his fall and saved him, and instead landing on the hard cobbles, the impact splitting his head in two.

Casting just a cursory glance at the Spaniard's body splayed out beneath him, Laurence

shouted to Nancy and the constables to come
up. Back inside the room, after seeing that
Christina was all right and ordering Nancy to
take charge of the frightened child and take her
down to the yard, while the constables bundled
Miguel and Maria out he went to Lucinda, who
still had not moved.

Kneeling beside her, he raised her head onto
his arm. She was unconscious but alive. A thin
trickle of blood oozed out from between the
fine strands of her pale blond hair from a gash
on her head. Looking down at her exquisite
face, he was shocked by her pallor which was
touchingly shadowed by her dark lashes. Gently
he picked up her inert body, standing and
cradling her in his arms, carrying her as easily
as if she weighed nothing at all out of the room
and down into the yard, ignoring the grisly
corpse of the Spaniard, his head spilling blood
onto the cobbles, not daring to think at that
moment how badly Lucinda was hurt. Not until
he felt the sticky wetness which stuck the sleeve
of his jacket to his arm did he realise that the
blow to her head was not the only cause of her
unconscious state.

Holding Christina in her arms, Nancy stared
anxiously at Lucinda, being held like a rag doll
in Lord Rainborough's arms. 'Will she be all
right?'

'It is worse than I thought. We must get her

to a doctor and quickly. She is losing a considerable amount of blood. Clear a way for us,' he instructed one of the constables while the other took charge of Miguel and Maria. Their expressions were sullen and tears were flowing down Maria's cheeks as she cried silently. Their shoulders drooped in sad resignation to accept whatever fate awaited them. 'A carriage should be waiting for us on the other side of the bridge.'

When Laurence arrived back at Metcalfe Hall pandemonium broke out. Margaret almost wept with joy to see Christina had been found safe and well but, on seeing Laurence's stricken face and the sorry state of Lucinda when her cloak was removed and the amount of blood oozing from a knife wound in her side, she knew something terrible had happened and sent for the doctor immediately.

Fortunately the wound in Lucinda's side was only a flesh wound, the knife having missed any of her vital organs. It had almost stopped bleeding as the doctor cleaned and bandaged her, but she showed no signs of regaining consciousness and he feared that the injury to her head was more serious. Only time would tell.

For the next few days Lucinda lived in a subconscious nightmare world, her mind too tired to think of anything but pain and death which prevailed all around her, in a darkness which went on for ever. She was afraid and wanted Laurence so much, for him to come to her and make her fear go away.

Perhaps if she had been aware of his presence in the room she would have been comforted, for he remained by her side almost constantly, waiting for some sign to tell him that she would recover. Her slender body moulded the bed-clothes beneath which she lay, her face ashen and her soft lips slightly parted as she breathed, her hair spread over the pillows like a pale, silken halo. At times a great weariness would sweep over Laurence and he would bow his head, cursing his own helplessness as he waited, praying for Lucinda's recovery, overwhelmed by a savage tide of love and anguish when realisation that she might die invaded his mind in cold waves, sapping the strength from him.

It was just after midnight on the third night when she began burning with fever and she groaned and tossed, threshing about the bed, trying to throw back the covers. Margaret placed a moistened towel on her burning brow and at last Lucinda opened her eyes, glassy and vacant, calling out Laurence's name in her delirium. It brought an instant response, for Laurence took her hand, bending over her, murmuring softly—'I'm here, Lucinda. I'm here,' choking back the emotion which rose inside him. Whether she heard him or not he had no way of knowing.

She rambled quietly, her fingers picking nervously at the bedcovers, but towards morning she grew quieter and less feverish and seemed to sleep peacefully. It was only then that Laurence rose and went over to the window, looking down at the street below which was just coming to life as people began going about their daily business.

His face was pale and drawn with fatigue, his eyes bloodshot and tired. The past three days, which had started with the disappearance of Christina, had been the longest three days of his life, but for the first time since he had carried Lucinda into the house a feeling of lightness, of peace descended on him, for he felt that the crisis had passed, that she would live now the fever had abated.

It was mid-morning when Lucinda finally regained consciousness. Laurence was beside her, looking down, and he smiled with relief when she opened her eyes, those wonderful, luminous violet eyes, clear now the fever had passed.

'At last,' he murmured. 'I was beginning to wonder when you would wake.'

Lucinda looked at him for a long moment,

trying to recollect her thoughts, wondering why she was lying there with Laurence sitting beside her bed. She felt a stab of pain in her side and a dull throbbing inside her head, then she remembered why she was lying there and the full horror of all that had happened in that room, in that house in Walmgate, came rushing back—of the Spaniard and how he had tried to kill her, how he had stabbed her with his knife before flinging her against the wall. The only memory that remained after that was of the moment she was lifted by someone's arms, and beneath her flickering lids she had seen Laurence, his face white and devoid of any expression save a hideous fear in his dark eyes, before pain had engulfed her and darkness had claimed her mind.

'How long has it been since. . .?'

'Three days.'

'How is Christina?'

'She is well, thanks to you, Lucinda. Without you we would never have found her.'

'And—and the man? Alonso?'

'He is dead.'

Lucinda swallowed hard, accepting this without any remorse for what he had done—for what he would have done to her if Laurence had not arrived in time. She did not doubt for one moment that he would have killed her and thrown her body into the Ouse.

'And Maria?' she asked quietly. 'And her brother? Where are they?'

'In prison—awaiting trial.'

Lucinda closed her eyes tight, feeling a deep sadness, for no matter what Maria was guilty of she wished her no harm.

'Am—am I going to be all right?' she asked, her voice weak. 'I remember so little of what happened.'

'The doctor says you're out of danger now. The wound in your side isn't serious—it was the injury you received to your head that had us all concerned. You'll have to rest until you get your strength back.'

Lucinda summoned up a smile and raising her hand traced a line across his face. 'You look tired, Laurence. I do hope I haven't caused you too much trouble.'

Gently he took her hand and turning it over placed his lips on the softness of her palm. 'You will never do that,' he said, his voice hoarse with emotion. 'I thank you with all my heart for giving me back my daughter—and I thank the Lord that he saw fit to save you. I could not have borne it if anything had happened to you.'

'There was a moment when I thought I would surely die,' she whispered. 'When I saw the knife in Alonso's hand.'

'Then there is a part of me that would have died also, Lucinda. I love you, you see. Never have I met a woman who inspires me with such emotions. I have endured all the torments of hell these past days so you must promise me never to expose yourself to such danger again. Do you promise? Otherwise I shall be forced to keep you under lock and key at Rainborough.'

Slowly Lucinda let her eyes travel over his face and her mouth softened as waves of great joy swept over her. Surely what he had said couldn't be true?

'So—you have made up your mind that I'm going to marry you?' she said softly.

'Yes. I will not allow you to refuse. There,' he said, his lips curving in a crooked smile, 'it is well that you understand the kind of man who will be your husband and, anyhow, you owe it to me after what you have put me through these past few days.'

She sighed. 'And here was I—thinking you wanted to marry me for my wealth.'

He frowned and his voice was deadly serious when he spoke, her hand still locked in his. 'No. I do not deny that your dowry will be welcome to help restore Rainborough—that Christina will have a mother and stability in her life, but these are only secondary issues to what is most important—which is that you will be my wife.

'The first time I set eyes on you in York I knew you were different from any other woman I had ever met. I wanted you then—even though I had no idea as to your identity. I was relieved when Henrietta chose not to marry me—for I had already decided that you were the one I wanted. I want you for my wife, Lucinda. I want you—all of you—to be my lover for always. If you were penniless, I would marry you and live the rest of my life in poverty—whilst being the happiest man on earth.'

Tears welled unbidden in Lucinda's eyes and she was suffused with happiness. From where she lay on the pillows she gazed wonderingly at him, scarcely able to believe what he had said.

'Oh, Laurence. You have no idea how much I have wanted you to say that. I will be glad to be your wife.' She closed her eyes, sighing with a deep contentment. 'I love you, Laurence Dwyer, and you will make me the happiest woman on earth,' she murmured, suddenly overcome with tiredness. She lifted his hand to her lips, breathing in the very essence of him. It was only a small part of the man she was to live with for the rest of her life but it would suffice for now. It would become a part of his love that she would feel about her whilst she slept.

Not wishing to overtax her strength Laurence leaned over and bent his head down to hers, placing his lips gently on hers. He kissed her very slowly and tenderly, without passion, almost as though he were kissing a child. When he straightened up she was already asleep and with one last lingering look at her face he went in search of Margaret.

Lucinda's recovery was slow and it was a further four days before the doctor would allow her to get out of bed. The wound in her side was healing nicely and no longer troubled her, and her head no longer ached quite so much. She was eager to be well again, well enough to travel, for she knew how anxious Laurence was to return to Rainborough before the roads became impassable.

Christina was giving Laurence cause for concern. She missed Maria terribly, which was to be expected, for she had looked after Christina since birth. Margaret did her best to console the child but it was to Lucinda's sick room that she always strayed, climbing up onto the big bed and seeming to find comfort in her nearness. Perhaps it was because her father seemed to spend a lot of his time with Lucinda but, whatever the reason, Laurence was pleased to see his daughter and future wife were growing used to one another.

Lucinda enjoyed Christina's visits to her room. Although she'd had no experience of children, the child was so adorable she experienced none of the difficulties she thought she would have in getting to know her. She liked the feel of her little body pressed against her own, taking pleasure in the fact that she genuinely wanted to be with her, putting her small hand trustingly into hers.

She was an active, inquisitive child and Lucinda would tell her stories, the ones her own mother used to tell her and Henrietta when they had been children on Barbados. Christina would listen wide-eyed with wonder and when she became drowsy Lucinda would sing her a lullaby and cuddle her as she went to sleep.

On one such occasion Laurence happened to enter the room to see Lucinda's cheek resting on Christina's black curls, her arms holding the child close. Both were asleep and a sense of peace hung over them. Moving closer to the bed, he looked down on them, enthralled by the perfect picture they made, grateful for the efforts Lucinda was making in getting to know his daughter, the poor motherless mite.

Ever since he had taken her from the only home she had ever known with her grandfather in Spain, he had had to get to know her and learn how to take care of her. Now he felt a strong sense of responsibility for her and loved her deeply. Smiling softly, well satisfied at the way the two were becoming close, he went out of the room, softly closing the door.

*   *   *

On the first day that Lucinda left her room to come downstairs, she was alone in the drawing-room when Laurence entered, having just returned from the Sheriff's prison where Maria and her brother were awaiting trial. His face was grim. Lucinda crossed over to him. She had been concerned about Maria, determined to do all she could to persuade Laurence to see to it that she and Miguel were released.

After a lot of persuasion, for Laurence had wanted them punished for all the suffering they had caused, he had finally acceded to her wishes, provided they returned to Spain, though agreeing with her that they'd had no choice but to do as Don Philippe had ordered, and that they'd had no intention of harming Christina.

'You saw Maria?' asked Lucinda.

'Yes.'

'How is she?'

'Quite distraught and frightened at finding herself in that place. You will be pleased to know that I have dropped all charges against her and her brother.'

'Oh, Laurence—I am so relieved. I have been so worried about her. Of course, I deeply regret what she did—but I cannot find it in my heart to condemn her. After all, she has loved and taken care of Christina since she was born. I dare say she will suffer from her loss as much as she will from Don Philippe's retribution. What will happen to them?'

'With Maria's suitability as a nurse to my daughter I could find no fault. The tenderness and care she bestowed on her was exemplary and I, also, deeply regret what has happened. But they will have to return to Spain—and face the wrath of Don Philippe. I shudder to think how William is going to take this when I return to Rainborough and have to tell him.'

Lucinda looked at him curiously. 'William?'

'Of course—you do not know of the strong feelings he had for Maria. Because of my marriage to Isabella, they got to know each other quite well in Spain. I was well aware that when he agreed to come to Rainborough with me, as my valet, he did not do so purely out of loyalty to myself, but also knowing that Maria in all probability would accompany Christina to Rainborough. Now do you see?'

'Clearly—and I remember Margaret telling me they were fond of each other. Oh, dear. Poor William. When he learns what has happened he may decide to go to her assistance— to make sure she has come to no harm.'

'I don't think that will happen. I have a letter to give to him from Maria, explaining everything.'

Lucinda paled when she thought of their sad plight, feeling she had no right to feel such happiness in her new-found love with Laurence. 'I pray that when Maria and her brother return to Spain, Don Philippe shows them some compassion.'

'That I doubt,' replied Laurence with some cynicism. 'Don Philippe is a man possessed of a fiery temperament—which I myself found out to my cost—and which, I suspect, after witnessing a tantrum being thrown by my daughter when I entered the house, she must have inherited through her mother.'

His words caused Lucinda to laugh lightly with a hint of mock sarcasm, looking at him obliquely. 'From what I am learning about her father, it is more probable that it has been acquired from him.'

He grinned. 'Is that so? And it is said that one does tend to recognise in others that which is in themselves—which is probably why I found myself irresistibly drawn to your charming self. Think what children we will make, my love,' he said, his eyes twinkling mercilessly.'

Lucinda flushed at the soft seduction in his tone but before he could make any more teasing remarks she said on a more serious note, watching him closely, 'Tell me about Christina's mother, Laurence? I know so little about her and you never speak of her.'

Abruptly his expression changed and he turned away, moving to stand by the window and looking out. Clearly her request to know more about his first wife had touched some hidden chord.

'Did you love her very much?' asked Lucinda quietly, apprehensive at what his answer would be.

He turned and in his eyes she saw pain in their depths as he remembered the beautiful Isabella de Silva. 'No. At least not in the way I love you. We had a mutual liking and respect for each other, that I do not deny, but our marriage was a mistake—we both knew that, but her father insisted on it.'

'But—why?'

'Because one night, after spending a hazardous few weeks chasing the French out of Spain—and taking advantage of a well-earned rest on our return to our garrison at Gibraltar, exhausted and carried away by the warmth and the wine of that country—and finding ourselves in the company of some charming Spanish ladies, my fellow officers and I availed ourselves of their services. Unbeknown to me, Isabella—who had escaped the strict confines of her home—was of noble descent, the daughter of Don Philippe de Silva. He was incensed with rage when he found out, accusing me of disgracing his daughter, demanding that I do the honourable thing and marry her.'

'And you did.'

'Yes. Had I known that Rupert was to die and that I would inherit Rainborough, maybe that might have complicated matters. But as it was, the army was my life. I had looked no further. Marriage had never been an issue, but if it was to be, then why not to Isabella? There was no opposing Don Philippe but I made it clear to him and Isabella that I would not give up my career. They understood this and accepted it and so we were married.'

'Even though you were both against it?'

'Yes,' he said, turning back to the window, staring out, unseeingly, his voice coming quietly to her across the space that divided them. 'But Isabella was very beautiful and I was fond of her and thought that perhaps, with time, we could make our marriage work. But my many duties with my regiment kept us apart. Our union was brief. As you know, Isabella bore me a daughter, Christina, and died shortly afterwards.'

'I see,' whispered Lucinda.

'The rest you know. When Isabella died, I was consumed with guilt because I had not loved her as a husband should—but I loved our daughter and was determined to care for her— even though I was apprehensive about bringing her to England and knowing that Don Philippe would do his utmost to get her back.' He sighed, coming to stand close to where she stood. In his eyes there was an involuntary tenderness. 'There—you know it all now. Do you feel better knowing about Isabella? Did it matter to you so much?'

'Yes. I had to know,' she said, lowering her eyes so he would not see the relief she felt in knowing he had not loved his Spanish wife as deeply as she had thought. For even though Isabella was dead she would always have thought of her as a rival.

Taking her in his arms and tilting her face up to his, Laurence smiled at the relief she was unable to hide in her eyes, but there was no laughter in his own as they searched her face. 'You little fool. You are as transparent as day. Believe me when I say that never before in my life have I known a love like this—and never will again. I love you, Lucinda, and only you.'

He drew her close, folding her in his arms, pressing her body close to his, his lips on her face, kissing her softly, seeking her mouth where they fastened and kissing her deeply. Trembling with joy within his embrace, Lucinda abandoned herself to his arms, returning his kiss with long awaited ardour and tenderness and twining her arms about his neck. They clung together as if there was no quenching their passion, their desire for each other growing almost beyond their power to master it. In that one blissful moment the excitement of the unknown was there — the joy and wonder which would be theirs when they became one.

When they finally drew apart, Laurence placed his finger beneath her chin and tilted her face to his, looking deep into the velvety depths of her eyes, darkened by passion. 'There will be no more secrets between us, my love. Tell me you are happy to be marrying me? That there will be no regrets — no secret yearnings to be back on that island home where you spent the best part of your life?'

Lucinda gazed wonderingly into his eyes, dazzled by the revelation of her love. 'There will be no regrets, Laurence. My life on Barbados is over. There is nothing left of that life any more but sweet memories to cherish — and I know the best part of my life is yet to come.'

# CHAPTER THIRTEEN

Soon after returning to Rainborough, Lucinda became the Countess of Rainborough. The wedding was a quiet affair, hardly the kind befitting an earl, but this was how they wanted it to be. Only one thing marred the weeks following the wedding: the death of Sir Thomas, but he died content, knowing both his daughters were happy in their marriages.

With Henrietta and Hal living at Burntwood Hall with Aunt Celia, Lucinda devoted all her time to Laurence and Christina, whom Laurence felt was still under threat from abduction from Don Philippe. Taking no chances, he made sure she was watched at all times.

Lucinda learned to love Rainborough Castle more with each passing day. She adored the old place and understood fully why Laurence had been unable to bear parting with it. Already, with some of the money from her dowry, the estate as a whole was beginning to benefit, and the castle itself was showing signs of improvement, with a veritable fleet of workmen both inside and outside the building. Christina was happy there, either running about the labyrinth of passages and rooms or playing in the wild tangle of garden. As yet Laurence had given no thought to employing a new nurse for her—Lucinda, with the help of Mrs Foley, who was delighted to have a child in the nursery once more, was content to take on the responsibility herself for the time being. It was an opportunity for her to get to know Christina a little better, although the two of them had become almost inseparable.

William, who had hoped Maria would have come to Rainborough with Christina, was subdued by her absence. Laurence had given him the letter she had written before leaving York but it had done little to appease his misery. A man of William's controlled temperament seldom gave vent to his feelings, but what Maria had done affected him deeply.

'I am grateful for the way you have handled the situation,' he said to Laurence when they were alone and he'd had time to digest Maria's letter. 'After what she did, you could have washed your hands of her completely and left her to rot in gaol.'

Laurence regarded him seriously. 'You above all people know I could not have done that. Content yourself, William. I realise that, to save her family from any suffering Don Philippe would inflict on them, she had no choice but to do what she did. She meant no harm to come to Christina. I could no more see her spend time in prison than you. Alonso Gonzalez, the man who died, he was the villain Don Philippe sent to abduct Christina. Miguel, Maria's brother, was only sent as added weight to persuade her to comply.'

Dejected, William nodded. 'I see that.'

'They have both returned to Spain, William. What will happen when they confront Don Philippe I cannot say—but I am sorry. I know your feelings concerning Maria, that you were looking forward to the time when she would come to Rainborough with Christina. Have you read her letter?'

'Yes. She explains everything and asks me to understand why she did what she did—and begs my forgiveness,' he finished quietly.

Unable to offer any kind of solace, Laurence had squeezed his shoulder in understanding and left him alone, hoping that with time his pain would ease.

After her wedding, in the bedroom which would henceforth belong to them both, Lucinda found herself alone with Laurence, with the beauty of Rainborough all around her. Often she had dreamt of what it would be like to love and be loved by such a man as he, but those dreams now seemed like unsubstantial shadows to the reality.

Although she knew the magnitude of her feelings she was anxious, vulnerable, excited yet fearful of what was to come. Divining her thoughts, sensitive to her feelings, Laurence took her trembling hands, covering them with his own to reassure her, drawing her close. She did not take her eyes from his, their feelings clearly mirrored for each other to see.

Laurence reached up and gently caressed her face, his finger deftly drawing the silken strands of her hair from her face.

'The life I lived until I left Spain scarcely taught me gentleness, Lucinda, but I have an earnest desire to be the gentlest of lovers this night.'

'Because you love me?' she whispered.

'Deeply.'

Reaching up, Lucinda locked her arms around his neck, bending his head down to hers.

'Then show me.'

At first Laurence seemed to understand her body better than she did herself. He was gentle and coaxing, but at the peak of their lovemaking he became a different person, the gentleness turning almost to aggression, demanding something from her which she felt she could not possibly endure, but she did and none the less was willing to give until fulfilment consumed them both.

Those winter days were almost like summer days, full of bliss as they got to know each other, their relationship unfolding gently. They talked at length, they laughed, they touched—and then there were times when they argued, when disagreements arose, and they would quarrel heatedly and Lucinda would accuse him of being disagreeably arrogant, insufferable and conceited. They were both strong-willed with fiery temperaments and Lucinda could bring Laurence to boiling point—but these disagreements added excitement and spice to their otherwise peaceful lives, making the moments of making up all the sweeter.

There were times when they felt a total isolation from the world in which they lived, when they would fall into each other's arms and make love with an intensity which surprised them both and which neither of them understood, when Laurence would glory in the nakedness of Lucinda's body and she would learn how it was to give—as much as she was capable of giving—and receive love. Laurence's desire for her was unquenchable, which she would return a hundredfold, with a fiery, wanton abandon, loosing any reticence she might have had.

She gloried in her present happiness which was in perfect harmony with everything around her—Laurence, Christina and Rainborough, with Henrietta and Aunt Celia close by, unable to believe that anyone could be so happy—but it was a happiness temporarily shattered when a coach arrived unexpectedly at Rainborough Castle one day during the spring, its occupants being a white-haired old man and an apprehensive-looking Spanish woman.

The man was Don Philippe de Silva and the woman was Maria, Christina's nurse.

With Lucinda by his side, Laurence met Don Philippe on the steps of his home, reluctant to let him inside. He began to tremble with a fierce anger, scarcely able to believe his eyes—that Don Philippe had the effrontery to come to Rainborough. Now the trembling had ceased and he was in control of himself. He looked at his daughter's grandfather and his eyes were cold, his hatred for this man like a physical pain.

Lucinda could only stare at the Spaniard, overcome by a turmoil of feelings, remembering the horror he had inflicted on her, that because of his insatiable desire to recover his granddaughter she had almost died. In her mind she thought of him as the devil who had tried to destroy Laurence. But seeing him for the first time in the flesh, she could not believe that this stooped, white-haired old man was the all-powerful Don Philippe de Silva.

'So,' said Laurence, 'it is you, Don Philippe.'

He was changed—no longer upright with the proud bearing of a de Silva, with none of the arrogant vitality in his now-lustreless eyes. His stature was diminished, his shoulders drooped and his head bowed slightly. It was as if something had broken inside him.

'You are somewhat changed,' Laurence went on icily, 'but I had no difficulty recognising you. You are a long way from Spain. Am I to understand that the purpose for your being here is to see myself? If so, then I am somewhat surprised, for you normally employ others to do your bidding—as my wife and myself found out to our cost. What is it you want?' he demanded

'To see my granddaughter.'

When he spoke in his strongly accented Spanish Laurence noted that his voice was older, strained, perhaps, but still the same.

'Why—what a reversal of the situation,' he scorned. 'Why do you think I should grant you anything when only a short time ago you sent a villain to abduct my daughter—which almost resulted in the death of my wife?'

'Then for that I am sorry. When I discovered my plan had failed—when Maria returned without Christina—my sorrow was made worse because I knew my grandchild was in a land without the comfort of anyone from her own country.'

'This—England, is Christina's country now,

Don Philippe. You have to come to terms with
that. Accept it. I am her father—and Lucinda,
my wife,' he said, placing his hand firmly on her
arm and drawing her forward, 'is her
stepmother.'

Don Philippe's eyes shifted to the young
woman by his side. He saw she was slender and
fair-haired, with a loveliness that could match
the dark beauty which his own beloved Isabella
had possessed. He nodded in acceptance.

'Aye—so be it. Gloat over my sufferings if
you must—it matters not. I did you a great
wrong—and though it is difficult for me to do
so, I admit it. But after Isabella died Christina
was the only thing that mattered to me. When
you took her away I did the only thing I could
think of doing,'

'By resorting to your usual devious methods
and attempting to have her kidnapped,' said
Laurence contemptuously.

Don Philippe nodded. 'Perhaps the death of
Isabella and you taking Christina from me was
the price I had to pay for the wrongs I inflicted
on others. My father and his father before that
became rich and powerful by devious means,
by the sufferings of others. Perhaps I failed
because that was the way it was—how I was
brought up by my father. Maybe if I had been
raised in poverty then I would have been different—who knows? I am no longer a proud man,

Lord Rainborough, and you will never know how much it has cost me to come here. But the teachings of my own father and the habits formed over a lifetime are hard to break.'

'What are you saying, Don Philippe?'

'Strip away all my money and power and what is there? What have I got left? Nothing. My life has fallen apart. People in my native Cadiz have become strangers to me. I do not ask for your forgiveness for the wrong I have done you—only your understanding. You are within your rights to refuse me permission to see my granddaughter but I ask you not to.'

Laurence looked at him hard, for if there came a time for revenge then surely this was it. But he could not triumph over Don Philippe now, feeling that if repentance were indeed possible for such a man then he would not divert it from its path by any actions of his.

The sad, even tones of Don Philippe affected Lucinda more deeply than she cared to admit. He was nothing now but a defenceless, vulnerable old man with nothing left in life save the love he so clearly felt for his grandchild. She was glad that Laurence saw this also and stood aside to let the old man pass.

'Then come inside. Christina is in the garden.'

Was it a trick of the light, Lucinda wondered as Don Philippe passed her upon entering the house, or were they tears she saw shining in his eyes? She looked towards Maria where she still sat apprehensively in the carriage, waiting to be spoken to. Smiling, Lucinda went to her.

'I'm so happy to see you, Maria. Come along inside. Are you here to see Christina? Or is it William?'

Grateful to her for her kindness, Maria stepped down from the carriage.

'Oh, Miss Lucinda—'

'I am no longer Miss Lucinda, Maria. Lord Rainborough and I are married now.'

'Then I am so happy for you. Can you forgive me for what I did? I am so ashamed.'

'Of course we forgive you, Maria. We understood that Don Philippe left you no choice. He—he did not punish you?'

'No. When Miguel and I returned to Spain without Christina, he became a changed man. Sick with grief. He ees so different now, you know. I came with him to see Christina. I have missed her so much—you do not know how much. But William I would like to see, also,' she said, unable to conceal the eagerness in her dark eyes.

Lucinda smiled when she saw William appear out of the doorway, smiling broadly for the first time in months.

'Then go to him, Maria.'

She left them to make their reunion in private, going to seek Laurence and Christina in

the garden where she was becoming rea-
quainted with her grandfather.

When a happier Don Philippe left Rainborough
alone—Maria was to remain at Rainborough
with William and resume her duties as
Christina's nurse—Lucinda promised to send
him frequent reports on Christina's progress—
and that, perhaps, in the future, a further visit
could be arranged. The gratitude in his eyes
almost made her weep. Laurence placed his
arm about her shoulders, drawing her close.

'People are so strange. Who would ever have
guessed that the rich, all-powerful, ruthlessly
ambitious Don Philippe could be brought to
such subjection by the love he bears a child?
No longer is he a man to be feared—more a
man to be pitied.'

Lucinda sighed, for there had been neither
exoneration nor forgiveness in the visit, but
with Don Philippe coming to Rainborough
there had been a kind of reconciliation.

'Yes,' she said softly. 'He's a sad man. But
I'm glad he came.'

Laurence looked down at her curiously.
'Glad?'

She nodded, watching the retreating carriage.
'Yes. Because now we can begin to build our
lives at Rainborough—no longer will we have
cause to expect him to snatch Christina from

us. Now the ghosts of the past have been laid to rest.'

Leaning down Laurence placed his lips on hers. 'You're right,' he murmured. 'It is time to forget the past and for us to start savouring the joys of the future.'

Lucinda swung back in his arms and looked up at him. His eyes were no longer cold as they had been upon seeing Don Philippe. Now they were warm and his lids drooped seductively. His lips lifted slightly in one corner.

'Have I told you recently that I love you?'

'Then convince me,' she murmured, pulling his head down to hers.

Lucinda adored this man, discarding all else. He eclipsed everything that had gone before. The serene, joyous acceptance of life as it had been for her on Barbados, and that painful parting from her beloved home he had eradicated, restoring to her a serene contentment. She had reached a happiness she had never dreamed possible and in that she was content to leave the unfolding of their future—their lives together—to fate.

# *Historical Romance*™

## Coming next month

# HIS LORDSHIP'S DILEMMA
## *Meg Alexander*
### A REGENCY NOVEL

When the Bath seminary closed, Miss Elinor Temple had
no choice but to take Hester Winton to her guardian. Their
arrival in the midst of Marcus, Lord Rokeby's entertaining
guests—which Elinor dubbed an orgy!—was not greeted
with good grace. Marcus equally had no choice, though he
insisted upon employing Elinor as Hester's duenna. Two
things became clear to Elinor—Hester's guardianship
owed rather more to family feuding than goodwill, and
Marcus was not averse to flirting with herself! But it really
wouldn't do to allow her own feelings to become
engaged…

# AN AFFAIR OF HONOUR
## *Paula Marshall*
### LONDON 1920s

Clare Windham had jilted her fiancé without explanation
and been ostracised for it. What malign stroke of fate had
brought the past back to haunt her in the shape of Ralph
Schuyler? It seemed her life was in danger, and Ralph was
trying to save her—but who could tell with this secretive
man, no matter how attractive he was to her…? Ralph
walked a fine line, and the more he learned of Clare's
integrity, the more he knew that, when all the danger was
past, she might never forgive him.

# SINGLE LETTER SWITCH

## A year's supply of Mills & Boon Presents™ novels— absolutely FREE!

Would you like to win a year's supply of passionate compelling and provocative romances? Well, you can and the're free! Simply complete the grid below and send it to us by 31st May 1997. The first five correct entries picked after the closing date will win a year's supply of Mills & Boon Presents™ novels (six books every month—worth over £150). What could be easier?

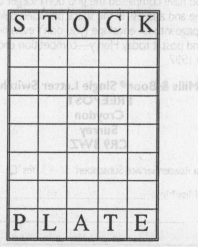

| S | T | O | C | K |
|---|---|---|---|---|
|   |   |   |   |   |
|   |   |   |   |   |
|   |   |   |   |   |
|   |   |   |   |   |
|   |   |   |   |   |
| P | L | A | T | E |

Clues:
A    To pile up
B    To ease off or a reduction
C    A dark colour
D    Empty or missing
E    A piece of wood
F    Common abbreviation for an aircraft

**Please turn over for details of how to enter** ☞

# How to enter...

There are two five letter words provided in the grid
overleaf. The first one being STOCK the other PLATE.
All you have to do is write down the words that are
missing by changing just one letter at a time to form a
new word and eventually change the word STOCK into
PLATE. You only have eight chances but we have supplied
you with clues as to what each one is. Good Luck!

When you have completed the grid don't forget to fill in
your name and address in the space provided below and
pop this page into an envelope (you don't even need a
stamp) and post it today. Hurry—competition ends
31st May 1997.

**Mills & Boon® Single Letter Switch**
**FREEPOST**
**Croydon**
**Surrey**
**CR9 3WZ**

Are you a Reader Service Subscriber?      Yes ❏    No ❏

Ms/Mrs/Miss/Mr _____

Address _____

_____

_____ Postcode _____

One application per household.

You may be mailed with other offers from other reputable companies as a
result of this application. If you would prefer not to receive such offers,
please tick box.   ❏

C6K